The Giant had brought disaster on the City and the good name of Chooker's family was tarnished. Chooker decides that the only way to restore the people's faith in her House, and in Mungith, her cousin, who found the Giant in the Mines, is to go Outside, find the other Giants, and prove that they are not all bad. And when Hemminal, the ex-Wilder and sister of the King, tries to kill Chooker in order to stop her, it only makes Chooker realize how urgent her mission is . . .

FRANCES MARY HENDRY was a teacher in Scotland for over twenty years. She has also run a small guest house which only had visitors in the summer, which meant she could write all winter. Until 1986, when she won the S. A. C. Literary Award for her book *Quest for Kelpie*, the only writing she had done was pantomimes for her local drama club—something she still enjoys doing. She also won the S. A. C. Literary Award for *Quest for a Maid* in 1988 and has had five other books published since then. Her first book for Oxford University Press, *Chandra*, won the Writer's Guild Award and the Lancashire Book Award. *Atlantis in Peril* is her third book for Oxford University Press.

Her other interests include history (until men started to wear trousers), gardening, embroidery, and amateur dramatics—especially pantomimes.

Atlantis in Peril

Other books by Frances Mary Hendry

Atlantis in
Peril

Frances Mary Hendry

Oxford University Press
Oxford New York Toronto

Oxford University Press, Great Clarendon Street,
Oxford OX2 6DP

Oxford New York
Athens Auckland Bangkok Bogota Bombay
Buenos Aires Calcutta Cape Town Dar es Salaam
Delhi Florence Hong Kong Istanbul Karachi
Kuala Lumpur Madras Madrid Melbourne
Mexico City Nairobi Paris Singapore
Taipei Tokyo Toronto Warsaw

and associated companies in
Berlin Ibadan

Oxford is a trade mark of Oxford University Press

A CIP catalogue record for this book is available
from the British Library

ISBN 0 19 271789 8

Cover illustration by Kevin Jenkins

Printed and bound in Great Britain by
Biddles Ltd, Guildford and King's Lynn

In the beginning, in the white tides,
Rassiyyak, the Great God of Fire,
Osiriyyak, the Great God of Rock,
and **Issiyyal**, the Great Goddess of Water,
made the world, and it was called **Atlantis**.
But the people of **Atlantis**
forgot to thank the great gods for making them.
The great gods were angered, and destroyed all the world
with cold and fire, earthquakes and darkness, hunger and madness.
But **Rammesak** and **Elonal**, a young man and woman,
were out in a boat, fishing.
Beliyyak the Dolphin God and **Bastiyyal** the Cat Goddess
led them to a huge cavern in a rock,
with light glowing all around, and warmth, and food.
Rammesak and **Elonal** said to the little gods **Beliyyak** and **Bastiyyal**,
'Thank you for saving us.
Please live with us and watch over us, but not too closely.'
So **Rammesak** and **Elonal** were the first Father and Mother
of the new world of **Atlantis**.
Many sixty-cycles later, **Mungith**, a child of Point House,
chose to go into the Coal mines for his adult trial, and found a giant,
and **Mungith's** younger cousin **Chooker** led them back to the City.
The whole City praised **Mungith** and **Chooker** for bringing back the giant.
But the giant brought a terrible plague from Outside the City,
and it was cast out and killed.

Atlantis

Atlantis is a huge complex of many caves underneath Antarctica, on the edge of the volcanic field which surfaces in the volcano of Mount Erebus. The nearby lava melts ice from the glaciers above for water. The tide enters through underwater tunnels and holes at each end of the chain of caverns, in spouts and whirlpools. Rising, it forces stale air out under the edges of the ice, and sucks fresh, cold air in as it falls. The people know only one way out, which they call Death Gate.

A luminous film of algae covers everything, giving enough light for their large eyes to see by. In addition, a few caves have holes up to the ice above, where dim sunlight filters through. These caves are used for breeding cavies, dodos, and rats, and for growing lichens. Lava holes are utilized as foundries and smithies for copper, bronze, and glass, and coal is mined. Many kinds of resins are produced. Shellfish and seaweeds, eels and octopus are farmed, and seals use these wide caves as a resting-place in winter. Friendly dolphins enjoy hauling boats for the Wave Family, for a reward of fish. The deep water of the main caverns provides fish, sharks, and sea mammals. Huge, dangerous wild rats scavenge round the City.

Time is measured by the tides. A day is two tides (about 25 hours), called light-tide and dark-tide—a memory of Outside. About half the people are awake during each tide, and at change-over at high-tides there is a general meeting time of about four hours, when they have their main meals—light-dinner and dark-dinner. They count in sixties, not hundreds; $60 = 3 \times 4 \times 5$. An Atlantan year is six sixty-days; actually 375 days, in the Outside world. So a cycle is the time it takes for the longest day Outside to go ahead, over the years, and return to the same date; about 36 years. Nobody worries very much; with little light, there is little use for writing and records. History becomes legend; what is forgotten, they say, is not worth remembering.

Atlantis holds about 8,000 people. They are small, mostly about 1.2m, tough and wiry, with large, sensitive eyes. Several have mental powers—telepathy, healing, finding, etc. Babies stay in a cradle in their parents' cubicle until they can walk. Then they receive a soul-stone, add a second syllable to their name, and move to a hammock in the Nursery. Children pass a Trial to gain the rights and duties of an Adult, and may choose to do so at any time after puberty. Then, before they marry, most become Hunters for two or three years, to gain teeth of, for example, rat, shark, or dolphin, which are Atlantan money.

A husband joins the House of his wife. People can change House by being adopted, at any age, into any House which will accept them. The Council of all the Fathers and Mothers, the heads of the 160-plus Families, decides all matters of Custom, which is their law. It is led by a King and Queen chosen by the Council. They are the judges and advisers to the Families, and as the embodiments of Atlantis must sacrifice themselves to the Little Gods in any grave disaster.

The Atlantans believe in reincarnation, so, although they mourn the loss of a friend or relation, death doesn't worry them much. Any baby that its House Mother judges will be a drag or a danger to its Family is sent back to the Gods at once, for better luck next life.

Rogues who repeatedly break Custom or Manners have their soul-stones taken away and are cast out of the Families to become Wilders, who live in lawless, brutal squalor in an off-shoot cave system; no one else goes in. They can earn teeth for trade by doing the heavy, dirty work, like clearing blocked drains or shovelling clinker from the lava furnaces. People judged too troublesome or violent are thrust out of Death Gate to the deadly cold of Outside, from where souls cannot return.

The Families of Atlantis live in Houses dug out of the soft pumice cliffs round the main City Cavern. The bigger, richer, better-run Families live in the three lower terraces above the harbour. The ever-changing Roof Houses, mostly small— Kelp is the biggest—burrow and squabble above them and in a few smaller off-shoot caves.

Each House specializes, more or less, in one particular skill or product needed by the City. For example, Boat House builds and maintains boats, and rents them to Hunters and the Houses which need them, such as Coal House, while Wave House trains and loves the dolphins which help to pull the boats. Tooth House breeds rats, small ones for messengers, big ones for food, and huge ones used for carrying heavy loads or riders, which are trained and run by Tooth's offshoot, Rat House.

Some of the Houses are excellent chemists. Gel House uses crab and lobster shells to make stiff and soft-setting plastics, useful, for example, for wounds, and makes a liquid that can be carried in a leather sack, but will temporarily soften stone—very useful for miners and builders.

Point House is one of the largest Houses, a Second Level Family, an off-shoot of Copper and Coal. Its mark is a tall chevron in copper and black, and its speciality is heavy or quality bronze-work—spears, knives, anchors. Its own off-shoot Families are all named Triangles, and mainly make small metal goods—buckles, hinges, etc. Points tend to be tall and strong.

Point Mother, Feelissal, married twice. When her grand-uncle retired as Point Father both her husbands claimed the position, but the Family insisted on choosing her son Distomak, her only child by her first husband. Point Mother has three daughters: Prentastal, calm and strong, the tallest person in Atlantis at 1m 60cm; Motoral, who loves the big hunting cats bred by Cat Family; and Chooker, small and lively. Chooker is about twelve Atlantan years old. She is a light-tide person, like Point Mother, and so is her older cousin Mungith, son of Point Mother's sister.

THE GODS OF ATLANTIS ARE:

Rassiyyak, GREAT GOD OF FIRE

Osiriyyak, GREAT GOD OF ROCK

Issiyyal, GREAT GODDESS OF WATER

Beliyyak, Dolphin God of men

Bastiyyal, Cat Goddess of women

THE MAIN PEOPLE OF ATLANTIS WHO APPEAR IN THIS BOOK ARE:

POINT HOUSE: **Feelissal**, Point Mother;

her son **Distomak**, Point Father;

her daughters **Prentastal**, recently chosen Queen of

Atlantis; **Motoral**, Chooker;

her sister's son **Mungith**.

COAL HOUSE: **Giffaral**; **Mylooj**, now a Wilder.

KELP HOUSE: **King Pyroonak**; his sister **Hemminal**, once a

Wilder; their cousin, **Wheerainak**.

GRANITE HOUSE: **Fixatchak**

SPIDER-CRAB HOUSE: **Priest Shevirrak**

RATS: **Peepik**, Chooker's pet; **High-Whisker**, riding rat.

7

THE FIRST LEVEL FAMILIES ARE:

Granite, Pearl, Coal, Tooth, Gold, Copper, Cavy, Fish, Fire,
Yeast, Ice.

THE SECOND LEVEL FAMILIES ARE:

Point, Glass, Boat, Dodo, Block, Crystal, Silver, Shark,
Harpoon, Wave, Bowl, Rope, Weave, Rat.

THE THIRD LEVEL FAMILIES ARE:

Dot, Drop, Spiral, Chain, Swirl, Square, Rectangle,
Pentagon, Hexagon, Octagon, Ring, Chain, Check, Key,
Cross, Saltire, Vertical Stripe, Horizontal Stripe, Slash,
Perpendicular, Oval, 4 Stars, 2 Diamonds, Eel, Bird,
Arrow, Loop, Heart, 6 Triangles, Hook, Shell, Fan.

The Roof Families are mostly small and irregular;
they constantly grow and fail, split and merge.
They are mostly named after objects or animals, e.g. Kelp,
Tube, Hand, Gel, Lace.

1

'Go stuff yourself up an octopus and squirt white!'

Over the bustle and noise of the busy harbour, and the boatyard beyond, Chooker's final screech echoed right to the cavern roof. She scrambled from the boat on to the pier. Everyone in earshot—which meant almost everyone in the City cavern—was grinning at her.

A gang of Wilders shovelling coal out of a barge by the quay straightened up gleefully as she darted past them, long plait flying, her wide mouth, pointed chin, and flaring eyebrows set in a glare that would have scared off a killer whale, her pet rat clinging tight to her shoulder-pad and squeaking in excitement. 'Manners, Manners!' one shouted after her. 'What a way to behave! What would Point Mother say!' They guffawed and whistled after Chooker, and then turned their jeering on the young Hunter abandoned in his boat. 'Oh, dear, what could he have said to her?' They made suggestions. 'Naughty, naughty!'

To hide his flaming face Mungith busied himself with coiling the harpoon ropes more neatly down in their tubs. Even a Hunter would consider before facing up to five of the outcasts of Atlantis, for no more than a few remarks. Best just to treat them with contempt.

But how dared his little cousin argue with him? He was an Adult, not a child any longer! And then storm off like that, embarrassing him! Eh, Beliyyak drown the stupid little cavy! He had a good mind to go right up home to Point House and complain about her bad Manners—but then, as Point First Daughter, the named successor to Point Mother, Chooker might just complain about him, and they might take her side. No, he'd ignore the whole silly squabble.

He smoothed a proud hand over his short brush-cut hair, the mark of a Hunter. He didn't need to pay any attention to a child; he was Adult and rich, handsome and stylish and— well, of course he wasn't vain, but he had to admit every girl in the City had her eye on him. In spite of . . . He'd not think of that. And Hemminal's was the finest, toughest, fastest, richest boat in the whole City. How dared Chooker criticize her? Even if he was junior in the crew, he and his mates were winning strings and tassels of teeth faster than anyone ever had.

The Wilders' sniggering stopped suddenly, as the tall figure of Hemminal herself stalked out of the Harbour-master's office. She glanced round the busy quayside, along the row of Hunters' Halls, up the high terraces of the City cavern, and nodded to herself in satisfaction. By the time she strode past them, the Wilders were bent industriously to their shovels. This was one Hunter who would have no hesitation in taking on a dozen Wilders, never mind five.

Looking unusually happy this tide, her hard-bitten face relaxed in a slight smile, she was carrying a bundle of harpoons and whistling quietly to herself as she jumped down into the boat beside Mungith and nodded towards Chooker's small figure trotting off up Main Street. 'Fleas in her feathers, eh? What about?'

Mungith shrugged angrily. If there was one person he didn't want to talk to about the reason for Chooker's temper, it was Hemminal! But the cold eyes were piercing, and she was waiting for an answer. 'Oh, just cousinly love!' he grinned.

'Eh?' The harpoons clipped sharply into the rack. Hemminal grunted, her smile fading. 'More to it than that. Tell.'

Mungith shrugged again, in resignation. Though he was as tall as she was, and a good deal heavier built, he hadn't her ferocity. She had been a Wilder herself for four years, until

Kelp House took her back a year ago. She would readily cripple an opponent to win the smallest argument; if you didn't want to risk a duel—and she never fought to a touch with paint-rods, or even to first blood—you didn't cross her. Her crew were proud of the courage, the skill and recklessness of their boat leader, and jumped fast to her orders.

'Eh, she says your brother listens to you too much, Hemminal.' Nobody ever used any friendly short name to this woman. He imitated Chooker's soft voice. ' "Custom says a King must cut his House ties. It's not right, to have the King's sister telling him what to do all the time. He was picked, not her!" ' It wasn't half of what Chooker had said, but that was enough to tell Hemminal.

'I tell Pyroonak what the Hunters think.' Hemminal grinned sourly. 'What's wrong with that? Balances what the Mothers and Fathers say. Time the Council listened to the young ones, not just the dodderers. Tell your little cousin that, eh?'

Mungith nodded obediently. Not that the Councillors, the Fathers and Mothers of the Houses dug out along the tiered terraces of the City, were all oldsters—Point Father, Chooker's half-brother Distom, was only about eight years older than Mungith's fourteen years, and their sister Prentastal, who had been chosen Queen the year before, was only nineteen. But true enough, they did seem to think old. It couldn't be bad, to have a vigorous young influence in the Council as well as the serious, sedate ones.

Hemminal was feeling the coils of leather ropes slung along the boat's gunwales. 'Not dry yet? I want to get out again right away. A Wave's just reported wild dolphins come up into Blood Dripper Pool. At least forty.'

Forty? Mungith whistled. That was a big school to slip in through the underwater tunnels from Outside. If they weren't killed, there wouldn't be a fish left in the channels in ten tides and then they'd raid the fish farms.

Hemminal nodded. 'If we don't move fast, the other boats will beat us to them. But there's no extra bustle—the news hasn't spread yet.' She felt the ropes again. 'Eh, these aren't too bad. We'll go.' She lifted the horn from its hook at the stern, and blew her own call; hoo hoo-oo, hoo hoo-oo, hoo-hoo-hoo hoo-oo.

By the third repeat, the rest of the crew were all in sight, blinking out of their room in the Hunters' Halls, leaping down the steps from the terraces or running down the curves of Main Road. Big Fixatchak, a Granite, lurched across the harbour flat from Granite House. He had been celebrating a wedding, but the horn was more important. Mungith wasn't surprised. Hunters' mates were their Family; and anyway, any crew member who wasn't in sight by the fifth call got a sore jaw.

'Right. Paddles out—we're for Blood Dripper. Dolphins. The Waves have called all their friends out of that area, so we can hit anything that moves. Mungith, fix those floats—and no kinks in the ropes, eh?' Hemminal nodded to the Boat House Harbourmaster to cast off, took the tiller, and steered for the low tunnel from the City cavern out to the main channels that linked the many caves of Atlantis. Her crew, some still half asleep, swung automatically into the rhythm of the long pull. No need to wake them yet; it was all plain paddling for an hour or so.

Mungith carefully packed the float bladders into the woven bone baskets in the bows and coiled their ropes beside them, tying the end of each to one of the newly sharpened harpoons. One of them was an oddity, one of the hard, incredibly bright ones recovered recently from hurt sharks and whales. It was whispered they came from Outside. He shivered at the thought. The Giant from Outside that he had found and brought into the city last year had given them some good ideas, like the wheelses which several Houses were developing to work hammers or pumps or pulleys—but it had killed over a thousand people in Atlantis with the plague of floo that it carried. He was glad it was dead. Many people blamed him for the disaster, including himself. Point House had lost a lot of respect because of him. He must make up for it. He'd never let anything like that happen again! He hated Giants!

Wave House's friendly dolphins didn't tow Hunters' boats, for they tended to join in the hunt in excitement and risked being harpooned. Even so, running down on the tide, it took little more than an hour to reach the entrance to Blood Dripper cave.

'Hunt places,' Hemminal ordered. Mungith came to the stern, where his heavy Point strength would balance Fixatch's massive muscles. Hemminal and her young cousin Wheerain moved to the bows as harpooners.

There was no point in creeping forward. The dolphins would already have heard them. Behind them they dropped a net of tooth-twine, with a weighted bottom and floats along the top, to delay and possibly catch dolphins which slipped past them; and then paddled gently forward into the pool. Its walls and stalactites shimmered with red algae, and the steady reddish drops from the roof that gave the cave its name dimpled the curling silver ripples where the big animals moved uneasily beneath.

'There!' Fixatch pointed to a swirl in the water as a dolphin rose to breathe on Hemminal's side. Her arm shot forward, launching the sharp Outside harpoon. Seconds later, Wheerain cast, with a shout of triumph. Already the first float had been jerked out of its basket to drag on the diving dolphin, and Hemminal had another harpoon in her hand. The paddlers dug and splashed, yelling in excitement as the boat rocked and jostled, heaved forward and sideways.

'Left!' Hemminal screamed, balancing her fifth harpoon. The bow paddlers reacted instantly, driving where she pointed just as a dolphin barged into the right side of the boat hard enough to dent the triple whale-hide. The craft jolted left, sliddering over the top of the water. Wheerain, stretching the other way at the end of a cast, toppled overboard.

Hemminal was totally concentrated on her prey. When Fixatch yelled to her, she ignored the call until she had made her throw, then swept spray from her eyes and glared round. 'What? Never mind him!' She seized another harpoon, and pointed across the pool. 'That way! Move!'

Mungith and Fixatchak exchanged a horrified glance. Wheerain was a Kelp, one of Hemminal's Family, as well as one of the crew; she should have dropped everything to pull him out, away from the dolphins threshing and charging through the pool. The ripping teeth or the sharp snouts, rammed in at full speed and power, could easily kill a person—they'd all seen it happen. This was bad . . .

Without a word spoken, Mungith back-stroked, Fixatch paddled hard and the boat's stern came round. It lurched in the waves, wallowing just long enough for Mungith to reach out a long arm and grab Wheerain's wrist. Fixatch leaned aside to balance them, Mungith pulled, Wheerain kicked. A dolphin, rushing below, actually shoved under Wheerain's foot and with a panicking jerk he heaved his top half over the gunwale. His legs were still thrashing in the water, but Mungith didn't dare do more; Hemminal was glaring, even aiming her harpoon towards them. He dug his paddle in again, and puffed with relief as she turned back to the hunt.

Wheerain hauled himself into the boat under their feet, gasping thanks, coughing water. He recovered in time to slide forward and throw another two harpoons before the dolphin school broke past the net and fled down the waterway.

Hemminal didn't say a word; she just pointed towards the nearest float. Puffing, they turned to the job of retrieving missed harpoons, and chasing down the dolphins which had been hurt by the spears and handicapped by the floats dragging on them, holding them back and exhausting them as they swam. It wasn't too hard to catch up with them and spear them again, finish them off and buoy them to collect later, with a bag of shark repellent dangling beside each to make sure they got it safe home.

They had harpooned thirteen dolphins, and although three managed to break free of the floats and escape, and they chased another one through four caverns before they lost it, they brought nine back to the City before high tide. It was a great haul, for only a few fairly minor injuries among the eight of them. Fixatch had a bitten arm, most of them had rope burns, and one woman had had a finger torn off, snagged by a jerking loop of line. As Hemminal's boat towed its long train of prizes into the harbour, the Hunters just setting out clapped and shouted envious applause. They would have to track the school now, and it would be alarmed and wary. Hemminal, as usual, had beaten the rest to the best of the hunt.

The tall woman leapt out of the boat with apparently as much energy as she had boarded it, and gestured to the harbour gang of Wilders to drag the catch up the slipway on to the quay. 'Due shares to Kelp, Eel, Bird, Stitch, Granite, and Point,' she told the Knife House Butcher on duty, paying her dues to the Houses of her crew. 'Then sell all the rest for us. The Loops are looking for gall-bladders, I heard. Give any bits that don't sell in two tides to the Wilders, and all the teeth in to the Harbourmaster for us, less three teeth each for your work, eh?' Ridiculously tiny beside the dolphins, the smallest of which was five times her weight, the old woman nodded silent agreement. The Wilders, grinning—the remains of nine dolphins was a good bonus on top of their normal pay; trust Hemminal not to forget her old mates—were already willingly hauling the first one on to the smooth granite cutting slab.

Mungith and the others climbed out on to the quay, stretched, rubbed aching joints and fingers, and waited apprehensively to hear what Hemminal had to say to them.

She jerked her head for them to follow her away from the crowd into the small room in the Hunters' Halls that was their home. There, among the litter of twine, leather, old boots, stained tunics, half-mended nets, burst gloves, she stood, hands on hips, eyeing them grimly.

'New style of hunting, eh, Wheer? Jump in and catch them with your bare hands? Fine. You can show us again, next time we go after killer whales.'

Wheerain grinned nervously, and then rocked and staggered as she cuffed his head, one side and then the other, with long, looping round-arm swings that made his ears ring. 'You're fined ten shark teeth—we could have got another couple if you'd not gone swimming! And stay in the boat in future, you dodo!' she snarled at him. He grinned nervously, holding his head, glad to have got off so lightly.

Then she turned her glare on Mungith and Fixatch. Menacingly, she picked up a harpoon. 'You disobeyed an order from your captain. True?'

Mungith shrugged and nodded, keeping his head up. He'd not show how scared he was. Though she'd not use that harpoon—no, of course not!—you could be put out of a boat for disobedience. But he'd do it again!

Beside him, Fixatch nodded too. 'Your cousin,' he rumbled. 'Our mate.'

That was the point, of course. They all relied on each other. Hemminal saw the agreement in the others' faces, and chose to back down slightly. 'For disobeying me—' Without warning she thrust. Fixatch gasped as the butt of the harpoon walloped him hard in the stomach. Mungith, hit next, had a second's warning and could stiffen his muscles in defence. Even so, he gasped, winded, his belly on fire. She could have split his guts there—it felt as if she

16

had! Fixatch was bent double, grunting through clenched teeth.

She stood and waited for them to recover, to look up at her resentfully, and then nodded to them. 'And for saving this guano-head, I'll split his fine between you. Five teeth each. You can use some of it to buy us all a drink. Right?'

'Right!' Fixatch grunted, hiding a wince. Rubbing his bruised stomach, Mungith agreed happily. The others cheered, slapped them on the back, and marched them straight off to the ale-stall at the corner of Main Road, laughing and joking, to be sure that they didn't forget.

Hemminal stood watching them go. Her own boat, her own crew, tassels of teeth—not bad, for an ex-Wilder! They were a good gang, tough and strong. Even that stupid young Point was shaping up well—if he could defy her to save a mate, he had guts. Most of them were older, coming back to be Hunters after working with their Families, to earn extra teeth. Wheer wanted a dowry to get married to one of the Shell House girls; Fixatch needed the teeth for drink, the fool, since his wife and child had died of the floo, but he was always competent in the boat. She'd heave him among the sharks if he let her down, or any of them, and they knew it. They jumped to it when she spoke. She'd stay on in the Hunt for a while; she enjoyed it. Better than her House's speciality, kelp farming, for sure!

But that child, young Mungith's cousin, what was her name? Chacker? No, Chooker—cheeky little cockroach! All those First and Second Level Families thought they were something special, and Point House was the worst of the lot, specially since their eldest daughter had been chosen as the new Queen. A word to Pyroon wouldn't be wasted. And no time like now. Half of Atlantis slept each tide. Hemminal was a light-tide, and Pyroonak was a dark-tide, but it was nearly high tide, when everyone was up and about; he'd be awake by now.

2

Chooker had slipped off from an errand for Point Mother to talk to her cousin, and was well scolded for being late home. At her next class, a cousin got through her guard and bruised her ribs hard with the bone practice knife. 'Lively as a limpet! You think a First Daughter is never challenged to duel?' the Weapons Teacher snorted. 'Bring your brain with you in future!' Everyone sniggered at her.

At the low-tide break there was a visit from Shark Mother and her First Daughter. Chooker hated both of them, but she had to be polite.

Then she fidgeted through Dwymit's lessons in Geography. 'What does a purple shade in Pink Thins show? Cold air, yes; and what does that mean, Veller? You should know . . . The high water pipes up near the ice may freeze solid, and Lichen Caves will have to conserve water. Good. What is in each Finger of Big Hand Cave, in order, Frat? Fire Fall, the Foundries, Resin House ovens and the Stinkholes where you may go for your Adult Trial, the small forges in Fourth Finger, and our own Point Forges in Fifth, yes, that's right, dear. Now, look at the map carefully, all of you. You see the dotted line from Fourth Finger to the Coal Mines? What does a dotted line mean, Traggul? Narrow, low, rough, or unreliable—good boy. It has to swing wide here round lava pipes, and it often collapses, but the Granites manage to keep it open most of the time. Chooker, sit still! Now, this map is part of the Seal Caves. Copy it three times—both high and low tide-lines, of course. Then you'll draw it from memory.' Chooker sighed, and concentrated. This was boring, but could be vital some day.

However, at last, an hour before high tide, she was free again. Right. If Hemminal could spend so much time with her brother the King, why shouldn't the Queen's sister visit her?

For a formal visit, she put on a fine cavy-wool tunic, replaited her hair tidily, and lifted from its hook her First Daughter pendant, a tall chevron of copper and jet on a copper chain. Peepik sat on her bed, watching anxiously. He hated being left behind. His long black whiskers drooped so miserably that Chooker relented.

'Eh, all right! I shouldn't, not when I'm going to the Royal House, but Prentast won't mind!' She strapped the carry-pad to her left shoulder, and bent down. 'Come up, then, you big lump of soft-gel!' Squeaking in delight, Peepik jumped up and hooked his claws into the netted pad as Chooker trotted out, her pendant bouncing on her chest. 'But we'll take the steps down, not the slide.' She mustn't act like a child, not when she was wearing the formal pendant.

Chooker had to wait for quite a while, as the queue of people outside the Queen's Office needing help or advice gradually shortened. She wandered through the entrance gap between the banks of seats of the Council Hall, to admire it.

The Hall doorway, with its wide carved bone doors, opened straight into the street. The ceiling was carved to a ribbed vault, painted white and gold, and the smooth mosaic floor showed a jagged orange star, representing Bastiyyal's volcano, in the middle of a blue and black spiral to show the whirlpools where Beliyyak lived. Carved pillars supported the circles of padded seating for the Mothers and Fathers of all the Families, a complete ring apart from the entrance passage at the front, rising in tiers to the two Royal seats high in the centre of the back wall. The door to the Queen's rooms was over to the right of the outer door, with the King's opposite to the left; and you went down tunnels at the sides under the highest rows of seats to the kitchen and store-rooms at the back.

At last the chiming shells sewn to the Queen's white curtain tinkled for the final visitor. Chooker could tell by the tone of Prentast's voice that she was exasperated. 'I'll speak to Egg House this very tide, Mother Tessival. I'll do my best, but I promise nothing. Good tide.'

Chooker rose from her stool and bowed politely, fingers touching her pendant, as Yeast Mother swept out. The older woman returned the bow, graciously regal, though she frowned at the black rat peering cheekily at her beside Chooker's ear. 'Point First Daughter, isn't it? Chooker? Yes. Your sister is doing splendidly as Queen. My compliments to your Mother.'

'Thank you, Yeast Mother,' Chooker murmured, and stuck the tip of her tongue out at the woman's back as she strode off down the passage to the main doorway. Then Chooker lifted the curtain and slipped in.

Prentastal was tall, the tallest person in Atlantis, and generally elegant and sedate, pleasant and calming to be near. Now, she was sitting on the window bench staring out over the Harbour, gently scratching at her new tattoo, the Royal ring of black and white checks round the House chevron on her left shoulder. Each House had its own glow; Royal House shone white, and the Point gold on Prentastal's skin had faded to a sallow yellow. Above her long white tunic, it made her look sad and weary. She sighed, and started to turn to greet this new customer for her help.

'Yes, she is,' Chooker chirped mischievously.

'What? Eh, Chooker! How good to see you again! And Peepik, of course!' Jumping up delightedly, Prentastal seized her little sister, picked her up off her feet and hugged her, before holding her off, puzzled. 'What did you say? Who's what?'

'Yeast Mother. A pompous snob.' Chooker grinned at her sister's laughter. It had worked!

Prentastal was already looking happier, more relaxed. 'Reading my mind, Chook? Little flea! But don't say it aloud, eh? She means to be kind, even if she is—well, bossy. Yeast lost all their children from the floo, and she's looking for suitable orphans to adopt in. Pity she'd never take a Kelp, they're trying to give brats away. Young Mother Grassipal's at her wits' end with them, she's just fourteen, but she was the only Adult woman left after the floo apart from Hemminal, and she'd never—' She noticed Chooker's eyes glazing over, and grinned. 'Problems, problems! Anyway, I'm glad you're here. I need a break from being Queen.'

Chooker winked at her. 'Don't worry. You're doing a splendid job. Yes, indeed. Yeast House sends compliments to your Mother!'

Prentastal laughed aloud at Chooker's imitation of snooty pomposity. 'Minx! A drink? Well, a biscuit for you and your pet? You never say no to anything sweet!'

She waved Chooker to the padded bench, sat down and relaxed beside her with a cup of cold spiced tea. 'Oh, that's good! Well, now! What can I do for you, Point First Daughter? You're looking well. How's mother? And Distom? They never stay to gossip after Council meetings. They're just a bit too careful of Custom! If it wasn't for you coming occasionally to tell me the news, I'd feel . . . Mother looks tired. Is she not over the floo yet?'

'She's worried about Distom,' Chooker explained. 'He's got no energy, that's why he often misses Council. The Silvers say it's his heart—it doesn't shut its doors properly when it beats. There's nothing they can do, apart from give him a new tonic. It tastes vile!'

She was glad enough to spend a while chatting. 'Motor's happy in Cat House, and thinking of marrying Jimmirak, one of their men. We've got another baby, Trik—that's three now since the floo. Eh, remember moany Aunt Naween? She's met a Hexagon widower, Twentithak, and asked him to be her second husband, and she's so much nicer now, you wouldn't believe it! And her first, Uncle Jorriss, he's happier too, so we all are!' They laughed together.

Eventually, though, the news ran out, and Chooker sat in silence for a minute, while Prentastal's smile faded. 'What's bothering you, cockle?' she asked quietly.

Well. It had to be faced. Chooker drew a deep breath and cuddled Peepik for courage. 'It's Mungith. And Hemminal. And King Pyroonak. And the Giant. And Outside.'

'Oh. Something quite small, then,' Prentastal mocked her gently.

The tension was broken. Chooker had to smile. 'Remember the Giant from Outside?' she asked. 'Bil, his name was. Bilwinstonbil.' She sighed, remembering the mind-twisting oddness of the huge man's thoughts, his crazy mixture of gentle and callous. 'You know what happened to him?'

Her sister sipped her tea. 'Of course. But I wondered if you did, Chook. Nobody ever speaks about it, but you're getting a reputation as a Senser, you know.'

Chooker shrugged. 'I'm nothing like as good as Distom, or any of Silver House. But I often pick up feelings people try to hide, or at least the fact that they're trying to hide something. People's thoughts are so jumbled that if they're not deliberately sending to you it's almost impossible to hear anything sensible. But I listened hard, and I picked up enough to work it out. King Pyroonak promised to let him go home to Outside, and then he and Hemminal didn't. Shameful!'

'Does Mungith still feel guilty for bringing in the Giant? Poor lad!' Prentastal sighed. 'As if anybody else wouldn't have done just the same!'

'He's terribly bitter about it. Silly dodo.' Chooker sniffed in annoyance. 'He won't talk about it, but it's burning inside him. Worse and worse, every tide. And he won't hear a word against Hemminal. Just this tide I tried—again!—to tell him what she's like, but he just got furious at me. He thinks she's wonderful, when she's cruel and nasty and still a Wilder at heart. And now she's coming in here every day almost, telling her brother what to do. It's not right!' She was quite excited, starting to raise her voice. Alarmed, Peepik jumped to the floor.

'Calm down, cockle!' Prentastal took the waving hands. 'I didn't realize Hemminal was here so often. That's not good. But it's Mungith you're worried for, isn't it, really?'

'Yes.' Sulkily, Chooker flumped down again. 'He's being a fool. And I don't want my husband to admire Hemminal.'

Prentastal had to smile. 'You've always planned to marry him, haven't you? Ever since you were in the Nursery together. Your names were almost a single word. ''Mung-and-Chook are down at the harbour.'' ''Mung-and-Chook have been raiding the biscuit jars again!'' '

'Yes.' Chooker's face showed her anger and distress. 'But if he sticks with Hemminal, I'll change my mind!'

'You might be right. If he does, he'd be a rotten husband, and a disaster as Point Father.' Chooker gulped. She had been hoping for reassurance rather than agreement. Setting down her cup, Prentastal hugged her little sister's shoulders. 'But he's a good lad at heart, he'll see what she's really like eventually. There's time yet for him to learn sense.'

Chooker sniffed doubtfully. 'Maybe . . . but . . . '

'There's more, isn't there?' Prentastal didn't sound surprised. 'Spit it out, cockle. When you take it into your head to set the world to rights, you really do a thorough job, don't you? What's in your mind? If I don't know, I can't help.'

'Well.' Chooker eyed her sister warily. She might take this

as being very cheeky, but it was important. 'I think the only way to make people respect Point House again and make Mungith feel better is to show the Giants aren't as bad as everybody thinks.'

Prentastal nodded. 'How? Think of their illnesses, and their terrible fighting and poisons, and all the things Bil warned us about. Only a fool wouldn't be afraid of all that.'

'But the King leads the Council, and he says what Hemminal tells him. And she doesn't want to meet the Outsiders. So we're all doing what Hemminal wants, and it's not right, and we have to do something about it!' Prentastal stiffened, and Chooker rushed to blurt it all out. 'We should go and find them before they find us like Bil did! Queen Sullival thought we should, and old Silver Father.' Chooker stopped with a slight gasp.

'That's for the Council to decide, not you!' Prentastal declared firmly. After a moment her face softened. 'Leave it to us. When you become Point Mother, Chooker, you can argue for your view. And there are several of us who agree with you. Yes, I'm one of them—I'm on your side! But we might be wrong, and this is very, very important. Atlantis could be wrecked or saved by what we decide now.'

'But you're not doing anything—'

'Maybe that's the right thing to do for now. Did you consider that? Once the Giants know about us, we can't go back to being hidden. But while they don't, we can always meet them later.'

'But they'll find us anyway! They're getting closer—'

'How did you—oh, you picked it up, eh?' Prentastal shook her head. 'I'm glad there aren't lots of you round the City, we'd never keep anything quiet! Yes, Tooth and Cavy Houses have heard odd noises moving about above their light-caves. Granite, too. Bangs and rumblings and a kind of grinding roar, travelling very fast. Don't talk about it, cockle, or you could start a panic.' She stood up to her full

24

height to impress what she was saying on her sister, and instinctively Chooker stood up as well. 'For just now, Chooker, let it rest. Yes you're sensible, yes you're clever, yes you'll be an excellent Point Mother when that tide rises. But for now, leave it! Why not talk it over with Mother and Distom? Be sure they'll tell the Council, if your ideas are good.'

'But what if—'

'Are you, still a child, arguing with the Queen?' Prentastal's voice was icy.

'Why shouldn't she?' A high, angry voice made them whip round. 'Why not? When the Queen argues with the King?'

King Pyroonak stood in the doorway, his long, narrow face vividly flushed above his white tunic. He was tall and thin, like all the Kelp Family, and rather resented being smaller than his partner in the Royal House. He stamped forward to thump on the marble table in the centre of the room and stare at her across it. 'Hemminal told me this fledgling, this fishbait brat, was trying to influence you! Is the Council to be run by children? You arrogant Points, trying to rule Atlantis to suit yourselves, eh? The Queen should help the King, not oppose me at every turn—'

'I uphold Atlantis, not the King!' Prentastal stated flatly, facing him across the table. 'When I think you're wrong, I'll say so, Pyroonak!' It was obviously a well-rehearsed, often-repeated scene. Chooker cringed away out of the path of the hostile glares.

'Conspiring with your House to bring in more Giants, destroy the City—' the King's voice was a barely-controlled hissing screech, and he was spraying spittle with every word. 'I'll tell the Council all about this, what you're plotting—'

Prentastal talked over him till he spluttered to a stop. 'Tell them that I met my sister? My young sister, only twelve years old? A child! Eh, what a fine conspirator! Go on, then, tell them. And I'll tell them why she came—because she was worried about Hemminal's influence on you. Your elder sister. Your Wilder sister. Which of us is more likely to be plotting, then?'

The King's mouth twitched as he struggled for control. Then he swung towards Chooker, frozen in her corner. 'Out. Get out.'

'And don't talk about this, eh? We don't want the City to know what kind of a King it has!' Prentastal sneered. Turning her back scornfully on the King, she patted Chooker's arm. 'Go on, cockle. I'll be all right. Give Mother and Distom my love.'

Scared rigid, Chooker bowed and scurried out. The King and Queen fighting, instead of working together—how terrible! The King's mind felt hot and jangling, like someone with hysterics. Was he often like this? How could Prentast stand the strain? No wonder she looked tired!

Outside, she jumped aside, fast. Hemminal was standing within an arm's length of the curtain, listening to the echoing silence inside, as she must have been listening to the quarrel. She wasn't smiling. Her harsh face was quite blank, but her eyes were raging.

Suddenly the door curtain lifted again. Peepik was kicked out by an ungentle foot to bounce off the opposite wall. 'Cursed rats!' the King's voice snarled.

Hemminal's face didn't change as Chooker snapped her fingers to call her pet. She picked Peepik up, edged carefully round Hemminal and almost ran to the street door.

She suddenly felt threatened, as if she was being chased, and glanced back.

Hemminal was staring after her. Quite still, not moving, not speaking; but the vicious threat in her mind drove Chooker racing out of the doorway and up the hill like a thrown harpoon.

3

Four days later, Chooker stopped dead just as she and Mother came out of Hook House, and announced, 'There it is again. Mother, I tell you I'm being followed.'

Mother looked up from her basket, to stare at her youngest daughter in irritation. 'Eh, my dear, don't start that again!' She gazed round the busy terraces. At high-tide changeover the whole population of Atlantis was awake, and half of them seemed to have business on the Second Level today. 'How can you tell? Who by? Why?'

Chooker shrugged. 'I don't know, Mother, I just know it's happening. There's always someone watching me, someone unfriendly. I can feel them. I can't catch them, I've tried, but when I reach out they always think about something else. But I know they're there.'

'Eh, you're imagining it, feather,' Mother said uncomfortably.

'No, I'm not. Really, I'm not.' Chooker stiffened slightly. 'Look up fast!' A girl peeking over the edge of the terrace above giggled and ducked back out of sight. 'That girl's one of them. You saw the green shine—she's a Kelp. There's always one of them about, or a Wilder. Always.'

Mother frowned. 'Eh, feather, think! There's a shoal of those Kelp brats and not enough Adults to look after them properly, so they wander all over. And we're having to hire Wilders to do lots of extra work in the City. There just are more of them about than usual, that's all. And if they dislike you, well, Hemminal is—well, was—one of them, and they've heard about your quarrel with Mungith, and that unfortunate squabble between the King and Prentast, all over her.'

27

'No, Mother, it's more than that. Hemminal's having me watched, deliberately. I know she is.' Chooker felt resentful. Why wouldn't her mother believe her? She knew what she felt. Someone, a lot of someones, were definitely thinking about her, constantly hostile.

Feelissal pooh-poohed the notion. 'My dear, why? Why should she? I know you don't like her—well, who does? She's scarcely cuddly! But to take the trouble to have you followed and spied on—why? What does she think you'd be doing that could interest her?' She shook her mass of braids till their copper beads tinkled. 'No, no, you're imagining things. Maybe you're just tired. You've been working very hard this year, and you had floo—maybe you need some of Distom's tonic, feather.'

'Eh, no!' Chooker squawked in horror. 'Anything's better than that rat-piss!'

'All right, all right! He doesn't like it either.' Point Mother laughed at Chooker's disgusted face, and tugged gently at her daughter's long black plait. 'Now, I'm going up to Equilateral Triangle House—Mother Syveemal wants advice about a crippled baby.' They both stood silent for a second; it was always distressing if a baby was so bad it should be sent back to the Gods for a new life. Mother firmed her lips. 'It's a Mother's duty, dear . . . You trot up to Two Toes Yeastvat Cave. One of the Obtuse Up Triangle vats has gone bad. Mother Vimmeral's going to scald it out before it can spread.' She smiled, rather smugly. 'We've never had to do that, not while I've been Mother. It comes of not cleaning out properly. But you should learn how it's done. You can miss the Arithmetic class, the Teacher says you're way ahead. Run along now, feather, and don't worry about Hemminal!'

There were now two sick yeast-vats, and Vimmeral had decided to clean out all her thirteen before all the Triangle Houses' rows were infected. From the gusher at the far end

28

of the cave Ice House had channelled boiling water to the City; on the way, it kept the yeast-vats steadily warm. Mother Vimmeral and the Triangle workers siphoned the scalding water into the vats, added germ-killer and scrubbed them out, scouring and rinsing until after six or seven changes of water the polished granite basins and the surrounding rock were glossy smooth. A pink germ-pad rubbed across the stone didn't turn green; that showed they were clean and sterile, and could be refilled.

Chooker watched conscientiously, told Triangle Mother that yes, she could certainly take a few bowls of good yeast from the Point vats to start up again, and was glad to escape. You could almost get drunk on the smell in the Yeastvat Caves when they were all healthy, but the stink off a diseased vat was sickening!

The quickest way back to Point House was down the curving flight of thirty-one steep steps to Second Level, just above where First Level tapered off above Left Bay. As Chooker started down she talked to her rat, perched as usual on her shoulder. 'I always wish there was a slide here. It would be a good fast one, you'd like it, eh, Peepik? But I suppose, right above the jagged rocks down by the water, it would be too dangerous. Not such fun if we shot off the end, eh? But it's so worn, it's nearly a slide already—'

Got you! The thought was triumphant.

A yell, 'Look out!'

Chooker glanced up and back. Big round red thing falling towards her head . . . jar . . . dodge . . . crash—ouch, her ankle!—splashing over her good sandals . . . smelly . . . shark-liver oil . . . slipping—Bastiyyal burn these worn steps—grab . . . no handrope . . . thudding, bumping down—help!—even smooth steps hurt . . . on a slide after all . . . silly thought just now—ow, gravel—kilt would be ruined . . . even sillier . . . legs skidding out over the edge . . . rocks below . . . something hit her chest . . . grab it—

It was a rope. It held firm. Frantically, so did she.

She jerked to a stop, dangling over the drop. The rope was cutting her palms, her wrists and knuckles bruising painfully against the curved stone at the edge of the terrace. She didn't notice. She was hauling herself up that darling rope like a cockroach going up a ladder, feet and knees scrabbling at the face of the House below her, till she got an arm and then her chest up onto the edge, kicked her legs up onto the terrace and wriggled and crawled forward, away from the rocks beneath.

As suddenly as it had started, the incident was over.

Well, almost. Still gripping the rope, she lay on the gravel that had helped to brake her, and stared at her rescuer, a Hunter, who amazingly was on the terrace above. He wasn't looking at her but shouting along the path, 'Dodo-head! Rotten codfish!'

He gazed along for a second longer, shaking a fist, and then hurried cautiously down the slippery steps to kneel beside Chooker, babbling in excitement. 'Are you all right, girl? It didn't hit you, did it? Nothing broken? Nasty tumble, that, eh? Lucky it wasn't worse. You could have gone right over on to the rocks. Point First Daughter, Chooker, aren't you? My honour to meet you. I'm Droogawfak, Hook House. Lucky I was taking the rope down to the harbour, I just had time to hold an end and throw you the coil as you bounced down. I didn't know if you'd catch it, but you clipped on to it like a lobster, eh? That fool of a Wilder!'

Chooker was gasping her thanks, but that stopped her. A Wilder?

People were gathering from all the Houses around, helping Chooker to her feet, wiping her cuts and grazes, tidying her kilt, exclaiming and commenting excitedly. 'Who dropped the jar? . . . Off like an arrow, naturally . . . Safe in the Wilder cave long ago . . . High time Block House replaced those steps, they're a menace.'

A woman called from the terrace above, 'Where's my jar of oil? Three seal teeth that cost me—what? What? Eh, don't blame me, I just left it at the door while I cleared the shelf for it!'

The babble grew. 'Where's the handrope? . . . Steal anything that's not tied down, Wilders will . . . That was tied down, ha-ha . . . Wall at the edge, I've said it sixty-sixty times . . . Feeling better, dear?'

'Yes, thank you.' Bruised and scraped all over, struggling to her feet, Chooker just wanted to get away from the fuss, safe home to Point House. 'I'm fine. No, no bones broken. Thank you, thank you! No, I didn't see who it was—I'd not know him again.'

She'd heard the mind, though, shouting in malicious triumph as she fell.

'Eh!' Suddenly she remembered. 'Peepik! He must have fallen on to the rocks!'

At the back of the crowd, a woman laughed. 'A black rat, with a copper collar? Is he yours? He's just climbing up the wall. Here, I'll get him for you.'

Peepik was like Chooker, shocked, bruised, and limping but not badly hurt. Secure in his mistress's hug, he whiffled his whiskers and cheeped, scolding such carelessness. 'Eh, Peep! You be glad I didn't land on you!'

Mother wasn't back yet but the Nurses were efficient. Soon Chooker was washed, germ-kill soft-gel put on her scrapes, and decently dressed again. Then she was told that Distom wanted to speak to her on the roof.

Distom was Mother's son by her first husband, four years ago chosen as Point Father. He preferred to be called his short, friendly name, rather than either his formal Adult name, Distomak, or his title, for the tiny, frail young man declared he never felt like anyone's Father in this House of large-built people. He was in charge of the trade of the House, bargaining for all the goods bought from other

31

Houses, and selling fine knives and hinges, spears and chisels, and all kinds of quality or heavy bronze work. Like most of the trading Mothers and Fathers he was awake in the dark-tide half of Atlantis, working while Chooker and Mother, and all the light-tide half who usually ran the internal affairs of the Houses, slept, and sleeping while they were awake and busy. However, Distomak didn't sleep well. He liked being awake during light-tide, for it was only then he ever had time to himself.

Chooker picked Peepik up and went to find him.

The halls and corridors of every House were always crowded and full of chatter, even if it was hushed to let the other tide sleep behind the thick double curtains of the dormitories. To be alone for a while, you went to the roof edge, where Custom decreed that no one, not even the Houses directly behind you, would notice or disturb you.

Distom's deep-cushioned chair was in its usual spot. Chooker coughed gently, to show she was there. Smiling, Distom beckoned her to settle beside him on the roof of Point House, her feet dangling over the edge and Peepik on her lap, and gaze with him round the luminous City.

Against the background silvery blue sheen of the vast cavern's walls and roof, and the blue-black shimmer of the water in the harbour below, the Houses dug out along the circling terraces gleamed gently. Framed by the carved and painted House emblems, their windows and doors glowed each in its own colour like jewels of light, strands of enamelled beads round the inside of a dish. Below Chooker's toes the triangular Point windows shone golden through tall copper and black chevrons. Below again, though she could barely see it, was the creamy glow of Pearl, about a third of the way round the curve that ran from the leaping turquoise curves of Wave House in the cavern wall to their left, past the round white-glinting windows of the Royal House rock beside the harbour in front of them, round

32

to the blue ovals of Boat above their boat-building slips far on the right, near the slope up to the Wilder Caves entrance.

Distom shivered slightly and blinked his deep-shadowed eyes. 'Your fall woke me.' A strong Senser, he was always affected by emergencies in the Family.

'I'm sorry, Distom.'

He smiled down at her. 'I was only half asleep anyway. Chooker, dear, I know you've been worried for some days. Mother thought little of it, but I wondered. And now this. Tell me all about it.'

He listened without interrupting. When she had finished he sat quietly for a while, considering, absently rubbing his chest. Chooker frowned; he really wasn't well just now. And now this, to bother him . . . She felt guilty. But it wasn't her fault!

Below them the harbour pool was split into three bays by the piers built out to the tall shafts of rock which supported the roof in the centre of the huge cavern, named for the two Little Gods who watched over the City—but not, everyone hoped, too closely. The right-hand pillar represented Bastiyyal, the Cat Goddess, who lived in the lava of Fire Fall and controlled the City's work, while the other was named for Beliyyak, the Dolphin God, who oversaw the food of the City from his home in the cold waters under the Whirlies.

Distom pointed down. 'That green boat, half-way out to the Bastiyyal Pillar, that's Hemminal's. Her crew tend to get hurt—one of them is sick in Silver House now, I believe.' Chooker stiffened—but no, she'd have known if it was Mungith. 'They're doing very well, though. Mungith has almost enough teeth to get married on already, in less than a year. Not at all bad!'

'Not all good, either.'

'Maybe not.' Distom nodded. 'You think she caused your fall? It wasn't an accident? You're sure?'

'Yes. I heard the Wilder thinking he'd got me. And she was in his mind—that she'd be pleased with him—'

'I know what you mean.' He could pick the vague feeling from her mind as she tried to explain. 'M'mm. The Kelp child could have heard where you were going. Cutting away the handrope on your quickest way back would be easy for the Wilder, and then he just looked for something to drop on you. The fact that it was slippy oil was a bonus. M'mm. You're quite right, Hemminal could have organized it.'

'But why should she?' Chooker puffed in frustration. 'It must have something to do with the King, and that quarrel with Prentast—'

'Poor Pyroonak, I feel sorry for him.' Unexpectedly, Distom chuckled. 'He must have expected to have everything his own way, she's so young.' Chooker's eyebrows twitched. He grinned. 'Yes, I know, but I feel ancient! And Prentast seems gentle. But in herself, she's strong. Not catch-sharks-in-her-teeth tough, like Hemminal, but effective. Organized and sure of herself, where Pyroonak isn't.'

He scratched his beaky nose, thinking hard. 'You think Prentast is lonely? You're probably right. Kings and Queens often are—that's one reason why few people want to be chosen. Now we've shown the City we're not going to be asking for favours, it's time Mother and I started to visit her. But don't worry about your big sister. She can look after herself. It's you I'm more bothered about, Chook. I'm sure you're right about Hemminal being responsible. But there's no proof—and why, anyway?'

Chooker sighed. 'That's what I asked you!' Peepik was fidgeting, and Chooker rolled him on his back to tickle his creamy belly. 'If I could stay out of her way, I would. But Mother's always sending me out on messages to the other Houses, to get to know the Mothers and the other First Daughters. And you know her. "So how long do we keep her indoors?"' Her voice changed to a perfect copy of Mother's high, emphatic tones. '"Especially when it might all be a nonsense. All youngsters play-act, and you know Chook!"'

'Do you mimic everyone?' Distom eyed her with interest. 'I didn't know that! Oyster House will have you on stage soon, eh? Do you do me?'

'My own House Father! What dreadful Manners! Would I do a thing like that? You'll say I take off Sea Anemone Father next!' Grinning mischievously, Chooker flirted her fingers and eyelashes like the fluttery old man. While her brother laughed till he coughed, she twisted Peepik's long, whippy tail round to let her pet snap playfully at the tip. 'Ouch! Keep your teeth to yourself, silly cavy! I wish you were a trained killer, like those fighting rats the Wilders breed. Or Motor's big cats.' That gave her an idea. 'Eh, could I go and stay with my sister in Cat House for a while?'

Distom considered it. 'No, it wouldn't work. She'd want to know why, and with her temper, she'd challenge Hemminal—and to the death, not to first blood, either.'

'And Motor's good with a knife, but I know which of them I'd back in a duel.' They nodded in grim agreement. 'Besides,' Chooker sighed, 'Hemminal would still know where I was, and I'd have to come out sometime. I'd have to go Outside to get right away from her.'

They turned and looked at each other at the same moment, in a second of wild fantasy. Peepik squeaked a protest as Chooker's fingers gripped painfully tight.

Rejecting the idea at once, Distom shook his head. 'No. I know you want to contact the Giants—and so do I. But Mother doesn't, and most of the Council don't. So you mustn't.'

'Why not?' Chooker was whispering. 'We both know it's the right thing to do. So does Prentast—she said so. Maybe that's why Hemminal wants to kill me, to stop me pushing for it!'

Distom laughed. 'You think you're that important?'

'Well, she did try! That's a fact, anyway. So she must think I'm important enough to annoy her, to be stopped. If she's against it, I'm for it! And when it's coming anyway—eh, Distom, I've got to do something! Or do you want me just to hang about until somebody gets lucky with an oil jar?'

They stared at each other again.

'If you'll tell the Waves to take me to Mungith's mine, I'm sure I can find the place where the Giant broke in. If I can climb out there, and find the other Giants—if I could make them understand me, and find out about them—'

'Too many ifs.' Distom shook his head. 'Too dangerous. And it's against the Council's wishes. No. And that's final!'

Chooker was ready to argue, but Mother came running up the stair to smother her in exclamations and fuss, and the moment passed.

But not the idea.

Chooker thought it over very carefully. Everyone she respected wanted to meet the Giants; those who opposed the idea were nearly all people she, and the people she respected, despised or disliked. It was dangerous; she could die—yes, face it, she could. But she could also win enormous honour for herself and Point House.

Or disgrace.

Or she might destroy Atlantis.

But the Giants would find them anyway, as Bil had done, sooner or later.

It would be a great adventure. She'd be remembered as a heroine in new Legends.

Or a traitor and destroyer.

Round and round her mind went. Yes, she should go . . . no, she shouldn't . . . yes . . . no . . .

No, she couldn't. Not while she was still a child, and all the Council—well, most of the Council—were against it. Really, no!

But there was no harm in finding out how to start, if she ever truly wanted to. Nobody could object to that, could they? She wasn't really going . . .

4

The first thing to find out was where to go.

All Atlantans had a good sense of direction, and could retrace any path once walked. Most could feel more or less where they were in relation to known caves; a few could sense new caves in fresh, uncut rock. Chooker was sure she could find her way from the Coal mine entrance to where Mungith had found the Giant that had broken in through the roof. However, though she had enough teeth to hire a boat to reach the cave where the mine started, no boatman would take a child without orders from an Adult. And who would help her? She couldn't go that way.

There was always the long way round, by that path to the mines from Big Hand Cave. Point Smiths went out there every tide. She could just turn up at the quay as they got into the boat, and say that Mother wanted her to see how the Forges worked. It wasn't a lie—Mother had said it, tides back.

But it wasn't quite true, either. Oh, dear, when you were doing something underhand, even for the best of reasons, you felt so dirty!

Not that she was going, of course . . .

But how did you get from that path to the mine tunnels that she knew? Or find out how the Giant had come into the ancient workings above?

No one knew all the tunnels in the Coal mines, maybe not even the Coals, but they'd know more than anyone else. So next light-tide Chooker excused herself from her Music lesson to do an urgent errand. Well, it was true, wasn't it?

Copper and Coal Houses, on First Level, were the founder Houses of Point. Chooker's grandfather had been a Coal

38

child, adopted out to Point because he was too tall for the small-bred House, so many of the Coals were Chooker's cousins. The women, who were the Miners of the House, were out at work or asleep, but the light-tide men welcomed her, gave her a cup of their special iced ale, and were delighted to show her their Great Map, a thick pad of almost-clear kelp sheets, layered above each other to show the different levels of the intertwined tunnels and caves. The Coals lifted the heavy sheets till they found the one they wanted. 'Old, old mine—here—far out, eh?' Though the men of Coal House seldom went near a mine, they copied the guttural speech of the women, who spoke in shortened phrases because their noses were so often blocked with dust.

Chooker peered through the sheets of the map at the dim marks beneath, concentrating as hard as she could, grateful to Dwymit for her boring memory practices. The tunnel the Giant had come through led outwards that way . . . she could find it. Casually, she put her finger on a dotted line that joined the mines quite near Mungithak's Trial cave. 'That's the path to Big Hand Cave? Isn't it often blocked?'

'Uhuh.' The Coal shrugged. 'Many falls. Hot, dark. Granites lay white stones, see road easier. Good idea, eh?'

'Splendid! Very helpful.' Yes, indeed.

Next—food. She certainly couldn't ask Mother! But Pie House had a stall down by the harbour. Chooker had saved sixteen shark and rat teeth from her birthday and Foundation Day gifts. When—if—she decided to go, she could buy a bagful of sausages and pies. If she didn't come back, she wouldn't need her savings again—don't think of that!

Clothes. Outside was all ice, and the Legends said that the draughts were terribly strong. She must take plenty of warm clothes. The Pie stallkeeper would probably keep a pack for her, if she could smuggle one out. Thank the Little Gods that a First Daughter had a room to herself, instead of a shared cubicle in the Nursery where the Nurses might notice clothes missing from a shelf.

She had it all planned. What a pity she wasn't really going!

The next time Chooker visited Prentastal, two tides later, she told her about the 'accident'. Prentastal was furious. 'Why don't you claim Adulthood at once, Chook?' she suggested. 'Then you could carry a long knife to defend yourself. Remember, you don't need to take an Adult Trial, cockle! The Council said so last year, when you saved Mungith. You proved yourself then.'

This was just what Chooker had hoped Prentast might say. Hiding her glee, Chooker spoke thoughtfully. 'Well, no, Prentast. Maybe that was just excitement, all done before I had time to think. I have to take a proper Trial, cold, deliberately. Prove I can be trustworthy and strong and reliable, to myself, as well as to the City. In the Stinkholes or something.'

'Maybe you're right.' Considering it, Prentastal nodded slowly. Many children took their Trial in the Stinkholes, in Third Finger of Big Hand Cave, enduring the burning sulphur stench for eight or ten tides. 'I'm not worried about you failing, but we mustn't invite gossip and nasty smears about Point House. We can't allow any hint of favouritism, when half the City condemns Mungith, and I'm Queen. Good thinking, cockle!'

Chooker grinned. This was permission to go. Near enough, anyway!

When Chooker stood up to go, Prentastal smiled down at her. 'Take care, now, and don't bump into Hemminal as you leave. I think she's in visiting Pyroonak.'

She was. When Chooker was half-way to the front entrance Hemminal's tall, strong figure lifted the curtain of the King's Office at the far end of the hall, but turned back at a word from inside. Nothing would happen, not here, but still . . . Chooker could get out before Hemminal saw her—no, maybe not—better hide. She slipped up the passage into the Council Hall itself, to wait among the seats till Hemminal left.

The harsh voice carried easily up to the rows of benches. 'Yes, I'll see to it. Tomorrow. *I'll enjoy it!* Don't worry. She'll have to go, we'll see to it. And you'll do that for me? Good. *Fool.* Thank you, brother.' Hemminal laughed shortly, a sneering kind of snigger, and her footsteps headed for the door to the street. *This'll shock them. Weak, Pyroon is. Like Fixatch and all of them . . .* The bronze hinges squeaked gently open and shut.

Startled, Chooker realized that she had been hearing Hemminal's thoughts as well as her words. She must have been concentrating really hard on listening, and the woman must have been very excited. Never again, please, Bastiyyal! It was like reading a rat's mind. A wild rat. Yuk! Hemminal running errands for the King? Eh, better that way than the other! Chuckling to herself, Chooker checked that Hemminal was well away before she left the Royal House.

On her way home, she stopped at the pie stall. Though slightly puzzled, the Pie shopkeeper agreed he'd be happy to keep a pack for Point First Daughter, any time. Chooker felt satisfied, excited, breathless—oh, that was just nerves! Had she planned for everything? Everything she could think of. Anything else, well, she'd just have to cope. That was what Adults did. She grimaced gently. This was really going to be an Adult Trial. Well, it would have been, if she had been going. She'd only have had to lift a pack from the store rooms—but she wasn't really going.

Pity!

Turning from the stall she nearly bumped into her cousin, standing staring blankly across the harbour.

'Good tide, Mungithak,' she offered, rather warily. What kind of temper was he in today?

41

He blinked, seemed to come back from a long way away. 'Eh, Chooker,' he muttered. His skin and kilt were dirty and he smelt of dead meat.

Chooker's caution disappeared in face of his distress. He was usually so careful of his appearance! 'What's wrong? What is it, Mungith?'

'Nothing,' he snarled.

'Eh, what a stupid! As if I couldn't see! Look, it's me, me, Chook! Whatever it is, Mung, you can tell me!' She touched his arm, and was horrified to feel how cold he was. 'Come on, what's wrong?' Could she read his mind, if he didn't want to speak about it?

Even as she thought of that, he twitched away from her. 'Leave me alone! I'm all right.' His face twisted, as if he was going to be sick. 'It's just—Fixatch died an hour ago.'

'One of your mates in the boat?'

He nodded. 'My partner. Fixatchak. A Granite. Big and tough and strong. You wouldn't think anything could hurt him.'

'And he's dead?' No wonder Mungith was in such a state. 'What happened?'

At once Chooker felt another puzzling withdrawal. 'We were hunting dolphins. The boat jolted, and I heard a splash.'

'He fell overboard?' Chooker was shocked, but not surprised. It happened. 'And a dolphin attacked him?'

'They're dangerous. If they ram you. His belly was hurt.' He jerked out the words, not looking at her. She could feel tension; he was hiding something. What? And why?

'He was in pain, but he didn't want to give in. He collapsed six tides back, and we took him up to Silver House. But it was too late. His liver was damaged. He'd been bleeding inside. And he died.' It was all true, though it hurt him to tell it. But not the whole truth.

Chooker nodded. 'Distom said that one of you had been injured.' Mungith twitched again. What was wrong with him? More than his friend's death! 'It's a pity Bil hadn't time to show us how his people operate—'

'Shut up about Bil!' Mungith's face turned patchy white and red, as if he didn't know whether to cry or faint or rage at her. 'You're always going on about Bil, Bil, Bil, the Giant—all the Giants—they're to blame—everything—the floo, and Prentast being Queen, and everything! Everybody hates me because of them! I don't want to hear about the monster ever again! It's his fault! I wish I'd killed it when I first saw it! I want to kill them all! You shut up about it! You're an idiot! A dull! If you ever mention it to me again I'll . . . I'll kill you!' He even lifted a hand as if he was going to slap her, before flinging away from her down the pier towards where the boat was moored.

'Sorry!' Chooker called after him, her jaw dropped in amazement at his unreasonable, hysterical outburst, but he didn't turn back. He was grieved, yes, by his friend's death. She knew how close Hunters were with their mates. But even so, this was dreadful. He'd never been as bad as this before. Calling her a dull—and meaning it? Ready to hit her, like a Wilder? Threatening to kill her?

She hesitated. What should she do? Go after him? He'd be angry.

Mother would know. Tell Mother. Yes, that was what to do. Mother and Distom would sort it out. But she couldn't leave Mungith, not like that—

'Excuse me, Point First Daughter,' someone murmured behind her.

'Sorry,' Chooker said again, absently stepping aside. Then she stiffened.

'Thank you.' Very polite, Hemminal smiled down at her. 'Hear you had a nasty fall a few tides back. Can be dangerous, even walking in the City. Can't it?'

Half hypnotized, finding it hard to breathe, Chooker could only nod.

Hemminal's smile grew wider, and she glanced along the pier. 'Poor Mungith. Upset. His friend has died. You heard? Hunting's dangerous, too. If your mind's not on what you're doing, you can slip. Badly. Lose your aim. Lose your life. Wouldn't want that to happen to young Mungith, would we? So no quarrels and disturbances to distract him, eh? No more nasty stories going round. And I'm sure you'll have no more trouble either. You do understand, eh? Of course. Good tide, Point First Daughter.' Radiating a venomous satisfaction, she stalked off down the pier, leaving Chooker frozen behind her.

Chooker gaped after her. Was that what she thought it was? A threat, to Mungith and to herself? Bastiyyal burn her! The sudden angry determination in Chooker's small face, jaw clenched, brows drawn to a deep frown above narrowed dark eyes, would have checked an attacking dodo cock.

She tugged angrily at her long plait. Hemminal had to be stopped.

But how? She hadn't said anything. Not really. Even if Chooker could convince Distom that the threat was serious, he probably couldn't persuade the Council just on her accusation to appoint a trio of Sensers to read Hemminal's mind by force; they hated to do that, for it distressed everyone, especially the Sensers. But even if they did, Hemminal would deny it, declare that she'd only been warning Chooker to take care, no more, Chooker had misunderstood, gone hysterical . . . Yes, Hemminal could hold that thought firmly enough in her mind to convince the Sensers. They'd not probe too hard, not when nothing had actually happened.

No. Chooker bit her lip. She was on her own.

If she was away, Hemminal couldn't hurt her, wouldn't

hurt Mungith. If she found the Giants Outside, and they were as good as she thought—or at least, if they weren't as bad as some people said—then Hemminal's influence would be finished for ever.

Was there no other way?

She couldn't think of anything.

And sooner or later, Hemminal would attack her again, out of sheer viciousness.

She had to get away. She had to go Outside, to find the Giants. Yes, really go. Soon. Now.

Eh, Bastiyyal watch over me, as closely as you like!

Along the pier, relishing Chooker's outraged frustration, Hemminal jumped down into the boat where Mungith was sitting miserably staring out over the water. From behind, her hand on his shoulder looked friendly; only he felt her fingers dig painfully. 'Poor Fix. Softer than we thought, eh? But the King will cover for us. We all stick to it that it was Fixatch fell overboard that day, and Pyroon'll say I told him about it when we got in. Anybody heard different, well, they just got the story wrong. Easy to do, specially when we were as drunk as we were that tide, eh? Wasn't a one of us could tell a straight tale, not to save our lives. But we can now, eh? Can't we?'

'Yes.' Mungith forced himself to grin and nod. It had been an accident, after all—Hemminal hadn't meant to kill Fixatch. He was a mate. So why cause trouble? They had all agreed what to say, and what not to say. 'I let Chooker think it was a dolphin. I'll stick to it.' He had managed not to lie, either. No one would ever trust a liar.

She slapped his back. 'Good man! I've arranged the Funeral Boat for next low tide.'

'What? Why?' Mungith was surprised that Hemminal would spend four shark teeth hiring the special red-canopied boat, instead of just two seals for red funeral flags for their own.

Hemminal shrugged wryly. 'Can't come. Job to do for my brother. I'll need this boat. Here.' She lifted two strings of seal teeth from round her neck, and handed them to Mungith. 'Send these to Beliyyak with him for me. And cheer up, you're dripping like rotten seaweed! Good man, Fix was—he'll be reborn soon. When I get back, we'll drink to his quick return. See you in a couple of tides.'

Mungith watched her stride away along the pier and turn, as usual, towards the Royal House. To his surprise, though, she passed the doorway and turned the corner of the huge rock. Her dark sharkskin kilt came into sight again round the far end, heading on past the boatyard at the end of Right Bay, and up the slope to the entrance to the Wilder Caves. No normal Adult ever went into the Wilder caves, not past the first cave to see the rat and cat fights. But Hemminal was different. She had been a Wilder, and anyway, nothing scared her.

Why would the King want her to do something with Wilders?

It didn't matter. Fixatch was dead. The funeral was on the tide tomorrow. He must tell the others. He'd feel better once it was over.

Eh, he could scarcely feel worse.

5

Chooker had been worried that she might be unable to sleep, and Distom would pick up her excitement and worry during the dark-tide. However, for some reason she slept like a rock, and Ice Father came in to argue about an order for lock gates, which left Distom so exhausted that Mother packed him off to his bed with a sleeping pill right after dinner.

The group of light-tide Smiths left for the furnaces in a clatter of jokes and laughter. Chooker should have gone to the Hall for her lessons, but she waited and watched until Mother went out visiting. Then, trying to look neither too guilty nor too innocent, she walked quietly to the door. Everyone would think she was with Mother. She hoped.

Holding the door curtain, she paused, gathering her courage. Could she go? Should she go?

Eh, stop going over and over it! Yes, she had to.

Under her normal tough shark-leather tunic and sealskin cloak she had squeezed on her thickest tunic of cavy-wool. Her pack of warm clothes was down in the pie stall. She had hidden a letter to Mother and Distom under her pillow with the First Daughter pendant—if she died, that shouldn't be lost to the House.

Yes, she was ready. Bulgy, sweaty, scared stiff, but as ready as she'd ever be. And thrilled . . .

Suddenly there was a wild squeaking at her heels. Startled, she jumped aside from a small black body jumping up to scratch at her knees. 'Peepik! I told you to stay in your bed! Silly cavy!' She'd miss the Point boat—

A boy ran across the Hall behind her. 'Eh, Chooker, you've forgotten your carry-pad—I'll get it for you.'

'Er . . . thanks.' Flustered, she agreed, and then cursed

herself. But if she left Peepik now, they'd wonder where she was going. Huffing in annoyance at herself, she took the pad when the boy ran up with it, strapped it on rapidly, shoved Peepik up on to it and marched out. 'Right, hang on there!' she hissed angrily at her pet. 'You won't like this, but you asked for it!' Besides, when she thought of it, the rat might be useful. He could maybe carry back a letter tied to his collar, like Mother's big message rat Veenik, if Chooker got stuck somewhere.

The Pie stallkeeper was busy with a crowd of Miners and a gang going up from Ice House to start a new waterpipe to the tin quarries. It seemed to take a year for Chooker to wriggle through to catch his attention, bouncing on her toes to peer over the counter. 'My pack, please! And . . . er . . . four big sausages and a dozen pies. Different kinds, yes, please!'

'Point Mother realized we do the best baking in the City, eh?' the Pie man shouted, making sure his other customers knew of the compliment to his House. He chuckled, stuffing the pies into a strong kelp bag. 'Twenty rat teeth, that'll be, Point First Daughter.' While Chooker fidgeted, trying to hide her urgent haste, he took the seven seal teeth she offered, leisurely gave her one rat tooth change, tied the mouth of the bag with twine. 'There you are, crumb—finest food in Atlantis!'

'Thanks!' Chooker called, already pushing out through the throng. She raced off across the harbour flat and down the pier towards the Bastiyyal Pillar, just in time to see the Point boat vanish down into the tunnel to the main waterway beyond.

Chooker almost cried with vexation. 'Eh, Bastiyyal! Why didn't you watch over me? Don't you want me to go?' A group of Hunters working on their boat looked at her in surprise. She made herself smile at them, as if it didn't really matter. At least Mungith wasn't there, to ask questions.

Suddenly a chorus of bright voices called to her. 'Eh, Chook! Good tide! How's Point Father?'

A column of Chooker's friends from the Third Level Triangle Houses, branches of Point House, were trotting on to the pier. Noisily they broke from their line and swarmed round her. 'What you doing out here?—Skipping lessons, eh . . . eh?—We're going out to see how the Forges work—Old Murrizal and Groonomak, they're taking us all together—Better fun than Custom or Geography—Riding rats booked for us all, great, eh?'

Behind them their Teachers were counting heads. Rather flustered, Murrizal greeted Chooker absently, her eyes busy on the bouncing children. 'Point First Daughter, good tide, now is that everybody? Stay away from the edge, Fortass! Twenty-eight—yes, that's right. We're all here, Groonomak, Blentiv from Right Right-angle House isn't coming, he has a stomach-ache.'

The youngsters were playfully jostling each other towards the water, peering down into the big boat waiting for them by the pier, giggling and whistling to the dolphins. 'Stop playing the dodo!' The younger Teacher, Groonomak, started to organize them down the steps. 'That's the Harbour down there, not the swimming pool! Fall in there and the sharks will have you before you bob up!' The Wave boatman looked resigned as the boat rocked and the children wobbled and squealed. His dolphins grinned and whistled—they enjoyed having children in the boat.

Maybe . . . Taking a deep breath, Chooker approached the other Teacher. 'Teacher Murrizal, could I come with you?'

'What? Come with us? Why?' Murrizal's eyes sharpened.

Chooker flushed and stammered slightly. 'I need to go to Big Hand Cave—I missed the Point boat, I was delayed and it left without me. Please, if somebody's not going, you have a place . . . ' *Take me, please,* she thought to the elderly woman as hard as she could.

Murrizal eyed her, and her big bundle and satchel. 'Is this a message for the Smiths, or . . . ' She started to smile. 'Are you going to take your Adult Trial, my dear? In the Stinkholes?'

Eh, yes, please believe that! 'I talked about it to the Queen yesterday.' It wasn't a lie . . . *Don't ask any more questions, just agree, please!*

'Eh, well, why not?' To Chooker's relief, Murrizal was nodding in fussy approval. 'Well done, my dear! We can always rely on Point House to do things properly, not to take short-cuts! An example to one or two First Level Houses, even! Certainly you may come with us. Not a good start for a Trial to miss a tide, not if Fire House are expecting you. Yes, yes, on you go.' She beamed as Chooker trotted down the steps to climb in among her friends, almost speechless with relief. Thank you, Bastiyyal! This was far better than going with the Smiths!

The Wave boatman whistled to his dolphins to nose into the padded rings of their harness. No one needed to paddle, for four dolphins could easily cope with this boat; they could sit back enjoying the ride, singing and gossiping, teasing one girl about a Tooth boy she fancied, pointing out faces in the rocks, whistling and clapping to the echoes. Chooker felt so full of excitement it was hard to breathe, never mind speak.

Each cave they skimmed through shone a different colour. Glowing algae on every wall changed in shifting, shimmering veils, reacting to small differences in chemistry or temperature as the breezes up from the lava or down off the ice blew along the caverns. The Main City cavern was blue and silver; Foundry Quay Cave was a yellowish green, light and soft on the eyes, and although it tended to make people look sickly Rat House insisted that the rats penned there liked the colour.

Two sixties of rats were kept here to carry people and

goods along the long, twisting tunnel to the heat of the forges and foundries at Big Hand Cave, and when the school party arrived their mounts were ready saddled. Chooker, as the smallest person there, got the smallest animal. He was a youngster, lively and playful. Everyone else, however inexpert, was mounted before her. 'Come along, Point First Daughter! Not scared, are you?' the Rat Groom laughed at her.

Her mount was tittuping sideways like a crab, teasing her, showing off his friskiness and agility, making her chase him across the cave floor. Everyone was starting to laugh at her. She had to keep up the reputation of Point!

Rats were clever. Chooker finally backed hers, tall as her chest, against the wall of a pen where he couldn't dodge away, put a hand on his neck and gazed into his brilliant black eyes. *Be nice!* she thought to him. *I have a pet rat, and I don't want to drop him. Go smoothly for us both, please.*

The rat blinked up at Peepik perched on her shoulder. *Ridiculous, small, silly!*

Maybe, but he's your Family!

Skee! That little one, pack-friend to High-Whisker?

Chooker chuckled at his insulted sniff. *Yes, truly! High-Whisker, be helpful to your little cousin! And to me!*

Mounts were bred for kindliness as well as intelligence, size, and strength. High-Whisker shrugged mentally, paused to let Chooker mount him, danced playfully sideways and back once more as she gripped the ring at the front of the saddle, and then decided to settle down. When the Groom told the mounts, 'Fifth Finger!' he scurried steadily along the twisting tunnel among the older rats.

Big Hand Cave was one of the few places in Atlantis that had shadows. The heat of the nearby lava dried the whole place up, so that the luminous algae couldn't grow on the walls and roof. Light came from the open lava of Fire Fall in First Finger, the furthest tunnel. Great silver mirrors reflected beams of dazzle across the black cavern, casting huge, eerie shadows on the walls.

Panting after their long run, the rats stopped at Fifth Finger Cave, where the Point Smithy was built. When their riders had dismounted, the rats stretched and moved off to join the mounts and pack rats brought by the various Houses working here. They were free now to groom themselves or snooze until they were whistled up to carry their riders home. Sliding off, Chooker patted High-Whisker. *Thank you!* He whiffled in surprise and pleasure. Few riders bothered to thank their mounts.

Peepik began to sniff and sneeze unhappily at the stink of rotten eggs wafting from the Stinkholes. 'Eh, you would come!' Chooker told him. 'You'll just have to put up with it!'

Little waterfalls called 'Bastiyyal's tears' glinted here and there, melting from the ice above the roof. By the basin cut under one trickle lay some cups and a pile of sealskin water-sacks. Hot and thirsty from the long ride, the children drank deeply. Chooker was glad to join them. Her two tunics were stifling her. Most of the heat from the nearby lava rose straight up through cracks in the roof high above, and cool air flowed in at floor level; but the rocks were still hot enough to make walking and breathing uncomfortable.

'Come along, now! And best Manners, please!' Murrizal told the children. They all crowded chattering into Fifth Finger.

Forgotten, Chooker looked at their backs. She could still go back . . .

No, she couldn't.

She had visited the Forges before, and knew her way around. On a side shelf there was a pile of clogs that clipped right over your sandals. Chooker hadn't been able to smuggle boots out, but the thick bone soles of forge clogs would keep her off the ice Outside just as well as saving

Smiths from the burning floors round the lava forges. Mine walls didn't glow, because of the coal dust. The cross-tunnel would be dark, too, with heat from lava pipes. She lifted a candle lamp, lit it, closed the shutters to hide the light for the moment, and stuffed a good handful of candles into her pack.

She crept out again, paused by the rill to drink as much as she could again, and considered; yes, she could carry a water skin. With her pack and food bag, and Peepik draped miserably across her shoulder, it was almost more than she could manage, but she'd need it if the path was as hot as the Coals had said. Or if she got lost—don't think about that!

Ready? Ready!

In Fourth Finger she sidled past the entrances to side caves with small furnaces where the Crystals and Drops worked precious metals and glass. She jumped when a light tap-tapping in time to a well-known chorus was suddenly interrupted by a crash of breaking glass, vivid cursing, and laughter echoing from several caves, but no one came out.

Stumbling in the blackness, she opened the side of her lantern. A white glint appeared, and then another beyond. The stones, thank Bastiyyal! She had found the track.

A sound behind her made her whip round—but it was only High-Whisker, following her instead of resting. She could sense his puzzlement, his curiosity about what this friendly rider was doing alone, so far from the normal people places.

Chooker seized the chance. Rats could see in less light than people; he could find the way faster than she could. This tunnel was low, but even mounted, her head was lower than most people's. Maybe this bold, eager young mount would take her most of the way, maybe all of it, where an older, wiser rat would refuse to go. She'd try, anyway.

Chooker tied her water-sack to the pack-rings, stroked High-Whisker's neck, and told him gratefully, *You're*

wonderful! Strong, and brave, and kind! You see the white stones?
Let's see how many we can find, eh?

Rats didn't understand about lava, not until they had experience of it. High-Whisker hadn't. He didn't know why they shouldn't go this way. He was young, and nosy, and reckless, and bursting with energy; as soon as Chooker was mounted, he stepped out willingly into the hot darkness.

6

Mungith didn't enjoy Fixatchak's funeral.

Not that he had expected to, of course. But sometimes, with a very old or sick man who had chosen to return his soul-stone to the Priest while still alive and go to the Little Gods to be reborn young and fresh again, or with a man who had died in an act of great courage, you could feel a satisfaction in knowing that his spirit would be welcomed by Beliyyak.

Not this time.

The Dolphin God lived in the huge swirl of black water under the blue glow and bone-shaking roar of the Whirlies, at the furthest end of the string of caverns. Respectfully, the crew clapped and stamped as Fixatchak's body was drawn down into the deep dimples in the centre of the pool. 'Farewell, Fixatchak! Go to Beliyyak in safety, and return to life soon!' they called. 'The Little Gods watch over you—but not too closely!'

Each of them threw a few strings of teeth into the water, to thank Beliyyak for his care of their friend. Mungith threw the two Hemminal had given him, and five of his own; a rich offering, but Fixatch had been his partner in the boat. And he felt so guilty . . . The others nodded approval.

On the return journey tension usually relaxed. Often people talked and sang Legend songs, setting the name of the man gone in place of a suitable hero of the past. Not this time; they travelled in sullen silence. When they reached the City quay, they stood awkwardly. What now? Their own boat was gone. Hemminal wasn't in their room. They looked at each other and shrugged.

'I'm going home,' Mungith said flatly. As the youngest of them he should have been last to speak, but after all, he had been Fixatch's mate. He needed a quiet time, a rest, to recover from the strain of the last few days.

The others exchanged glances. 'Yes—me, too—I'm going for a drink—and me . . . ' They trickled out.

Wheerainak hung back. 'Er . . . maybe going home isn't such a good idea.'

'What?' Mungith stared.

'Well, everybody knows Distom, and that nosy little cousin of yours.' Wheerainak grinned, malicious and shifty. 'Hemmin says if they start sensing there was more to Fix's death than people know, they'll winkle out the whole truth. Won't they? And then Hemmin'll be in trouble with the softies, not just for hitting Fix but for covering up. You'll be in trouble too, for helping. We all will—all your mates.'

Mungith stared at him. Everybody despised a liar. 'I didn't lie, Wheerain!'

Wheerainak sniggered. 'Didn't tell the truth, neither—not all of it!'

'But—will I ever be able to go home, then?'

'When it's all died down, sure. Hemmin says it could be a good while, though.' Wheerainak slapped Mungith's shoulder. 'You've always got us! Want to come home with me? Always room in Kelp House for a pal—maybe on the floor, but it's cosy!'

Share a pad with Kelps, crawling with lice and fleas? Mungith shuddered; but it was better than staying alone in the litter of the Hunters' Hall room. 'Thanks.'

They started off across the harbour flat towards the slope of Main Road. Mungith's shoulders drooped wearily. Not go home, not for years, maybe? What about his hopes of marrying Chooker, and becoming next Point Father? If they found out he'd helped deceive the City, they'd never have him. Never. What had he got himself into?

Behind him, Point Mother's voice rose urgently, calling his name. 'Mung! Mungith! Have you seen Chook?' His aunt was running towards him from the Royal House, careless of the stares from everyone around. 'Have you? Seen her? Wake up, Mung! Chooker! Do you know where she is?'

Dully, Mungith shook his head again. Who cared?

'She hasn't been in the House all tide! I spent the tide at Gold House, and when I got home I found she'd missed all her lessons, and nobody worried because they thought she was out with me. She's not with Prentast either. Where can she be?'

From a boat in the water below where they stood, a head rose as a Hunter stood up. 'Point Mother? You're looking for your First Daughter?' He smiled reassuringly. 'She went off in a boat with a party of youngsters. Up to Big Hand.'

'What?' Mother's face was desperately worried. 'But why, under the roof?'

The Hunter pointed. 'There's one of our youngsters from the boat. She'll know. Hey, Luffine! Come here a minute!'

The girl stared, and trotted over to bow to Point Mother. 'Good tide—'

'Where's Chooker?' Mother interrupted, not waiting for normal courtesy. 'She went to Big Hand with you? Did she come back with you?'

The girl looked puzzled. 'Why, no, Point Mother. She went to the Stinkholes, to take her Adult Trial.'

Mother's jaw dropped. 'Adult Trial? Without telling me, without any preparation, without a proper Farewell? But she knew I wouldn't approve—eh, Bastiyyal, surely she wouldn't?'

'Didn't need to, either, did she?' The Hunter grinned. 'Eh, that's a grand girl for you! You'd have stopped her, eh? Won't take any concessions, that girl! Never the easy way out for her! She's a credit to Point!' He called the news to his friends. 'Point First Daughter—yes, Chooker—she's gone off for her Adult Trial without telling her mother! Talk about guts, eh? Real little gold nugget!'

Mungith glowered. Beliyyak drown Chooker, showing off like this—just like her!

The news spread through the growing group in a murmur of approval and applause, and Mother began to look less strained. She clutched Mungith's arm, beginning to enjoy the drama. 'Help me home, Mungith, my dear. I'll have to tell Distom, and he's not well, he'll be in such a state! Eh, what a silly little chick! But brave, supremely brave—a true Point! Eh, my heart will burst with this distress!' She laid a melodramatic hand on her chest. 'My child, my youngest daughter, my baby! And how am I to tell my son, eh?' She looked round, gathering sympathy from her audience before turning away with a sob of emotion. 'Come up with me, help me! I need an arm to lean on in case I collapse!'

Wheerain, at Mungith's shoulder, shook his head in warning, but Mungith paid him no heed. He could scarcely refuse, even though he felt fairly sure his aunt could have carried him up the road as easily as he could carry her. You didn't argue with a Mother. And if Distom wasn't well, neither he nor Chooker would be there . . .

Distom was waiting for them at the door, shaky but driven by worry, with every other awake member of Point House from the babies not yet in the Nursery to the oldsters. 'Well?' he demanded. 'Where is she? I can't feel her anywhere in the City.'

'Slipped off to take her Adult Trial, it seems. In the Stinkholes.' Now that she needed to soothe her son and her House, Mother's dramatics were quickly replaced by calm and practicality. 'You should be in your bed, my dear. It will be all right. She's not totally stupid, I've no doubt she has arranged something, but if she hasn't raided the kitchens I

58

can send her food, and Fire House look after the children well—'

'No.' The coldness of Distom's tone stopped her dead, and brought Mungith's head up fast. 'There's more to it than that. I know there is.' He swung towards the passage to the First Daughter's room, but staggered. 'Eh, this weakness!' he cried in angry frustration. 'Dwymit, look through her room. See if anything is missing. Any clothes.'

Mother already had an arm round him, and was signalling to two of the older children to bring up his big soft chair. He sank into it reluctantly just as old Dwymit hurried back. 'Look!' she gasped. 'A letter for you, Mother, and her pendant!'

Ripping open the ribbons of Chooker's note-pad, Mother opened the double leaves of thin bone. She looked round at the agitated faces, and read aloud the short message written on the soft-gel coating on the inside. 'Mother, apology of worry. I go Outside, I tell Distom. I bring honour to Point. Love to Family, to Mungith. Chooker, Point First Daughter.'

Slowly, everyone looked at Distom. Mother spoke for them all. 'Well?'

The little man lay back on his cushions and sighed. 'She talked about this some days ago, and I told her to forget it. I promise you, Mother, I strictly forbade it. But she has gone anyway, just as she planned.' He drew a deep breath, as if he was carrying a heavy weight. 'She's gone along the path between Big Hand and the Mines, to find the place where Mungith's Giant broke in, to try to get out the same way, to meet the Giants Outside.'

He had expected an outcry, but not the chorus of screams and shrieking that greeted his announcement. It was a long time before even Mother's piercing voice could make itself heard, to demand approximate silence, and then the whole story of that talk on the roof. But at last, when they had all the facts, Distom nodded to one of the boys. 'Bring me the

red jar of mind-reach pills, Traggal. Top shelf in the Office.'
He raised a hand to Mother. 'I must! I know, they're
dangerous, and I'm not well, but—'

'This once I'm not stopping you,' she snorted, hiding her
distress. 'You'll go to bed right after, with another sleep pill,
but yes, try to reach her now.'

Distom swallowed one of the soft pills and lay back,
staring at the mosaics on the ceiling. The Hall stilled. His
eyes glazed as the pill increased his power, let him drive
his mind outwards, calling for Chooker, seeking any trace
of her.

Big Hand Cave . . . As he expected, nothing in the
Stinkholes . . . The watchmen guarding the valuable tools
and work left in the Finger Caves, they knew nothing . . .
Nor the Wilder clear-up gangs . . . Nor the Fires cleaning
the lava spouts . . .

Out towards the Mines . . . Blankness . . . Hard to think
into nothing, into rock . . . A glimmer of thought, a
flicker . . .

'Found her,' he sighed. His white face flushed. 'She's
well . . . hot, tired, bruised . . . riding . . . no, walking,
but a rat with her . . . ' Fighting to command the hysterical
energy of the mind-reach pill swamping his weakness, he
called out to her. *Chooker, stop! Come back! You mustn't do this!*

She heard him, but he could put no force into his
commands. *I can't stop,* she told him. *The old queen told me
we should do this. I'm sorry, Distom. Tell everyone I love them.*

'We know that!' In distress, he spoke his thoughts aloud.

'Know what?' Mother demanded. 'Order her to come back
at once! You're Point Father—she must come back! She
must! She can't go on, it's too dangerous! And what will
the Council say? They'll throw her out of Death Gate!'

But when Distom tried to reach Chooker again, he
couldn't. The pill was driving too fast for his sick brain to
master; he was twitching, trembling, desperately trying to

steady the whirl, not to be overwhelmed by the anxious minds of everyone in the Hall. Mother and the rest held him steady as he heaved and fought, struggling for control and breath, his heart beating to shake him.

Mother slipped a sleep pill into his mouth, and snapped, 'Swallow. Distom, swallow!' He obeyed his mother's voice, automatically. As the pill began to work his mind slowed down, but by the time he could think more or less straight, he was too exhausted to try to reach Chooker again.

He blinked up at the anxious faces. 'She's safe, for the moment.' His voice was a dry whisper. 'Hasn't reached the mines yet. Maybe someone could get there first and head her off?'

'Yes!' Mother leapt at the idea. While Distom collapsed in his chair, she stared round imperiously. 'Mungith, you have a boat, you can go—Mungith? Mung? Where is he?'

One of the children answered her nervously. 'Mother, he's already gone.'

7

Mungith's passionate fury carried him like a lava wave into Coal House, where the shift about to go out to the mines was horrified to hear what Chooker was doing. 'Meet Giants? Never! Head her off? Yes,' Coal Mother instantly agreed. 'Giffaral, you're Chief Miner there. Fast canoe. Others will follow.' Without a word, Giffaral shot out of the door.

They raced across to the harbour. One of Mungith's strings of teeth, worn for the funeral, came in handy to hire a light message canoe with two dolphins, and he simply tossed the rest of the cluttering, clattering tassels on to his bed in the Hunters' Halls. If Wilders slipped in and stole the lot, he'd blame Chooker!

Returning to the place where he had been trapped would have been a terror if Mungith had allowed himself to think about it as the canoe raced out through the maze of channels and locks, so he didn't. He stoked up his rage to swamp his fear. Attack? Rubbish! Chooker was always slandering Hemminal. Stupid little . . . little girl, risking the whole City, just to show off! He'd stop her! Beliyyak drown all Giants!

At the mine entrance, he tugged on heavy boots and the reinforced leather jerkin and helmet that would protect his skull and spine, slung a sausage of glow-tube round his neck, and just as he had done for his Trial the year before dived after Giffaral into the black of the low tunnels. Soon his legs and neck were aching violently, his neck, back, and head ringing from bumping the rock roof. It was all extra that Chooker owed him for, extra aggravation, an extra source of rage. He fed his temper with his aches, and his plans for revenge; what he'd say to her—what he'd do— he'd slap her so hard—he'd kill her!

Like Fixatch.

No, not like that!

Some of the venom drained away.

At last they came to the old working whose roof the Giant had broken through from even more ancient workings above. Thankfully Mungith sat down, taking off his helmet and rubbing his cramping thigh muscles. Eh, he remembered this place too well! The Giant had lain just here. And like a fool he'd treated it like a friend. He'd not make that mistake again. Nor let Chooker, either!

'No sign. Chooker not been here.' Giffaral was looking round. 'Maybe misunderstood maps, or turned wrong way—easy to do. Or stuck in path.' She thought for a moment. 'I go to path entrance. You stay here. Catch if I miss her. Always ways round, eh? If not arrived yet, when rest come, we go look for her. Yes?'

Stay here, alone? Mungith gritted his teeth. 'Yes!'

But when the clack of her boots trotted off into the distance, he felt deserted. She might never come back—the roof would fall again—Chooker would be lost—

This panic was silly. Nothing stopped Chooker, once she had her mind set on something. Relentless as the tide. She'd come, eventually. And he could find his way back if he had to. He wasn't trapped this time.

But it was dark, and lonely . . .

It was dark for Chooker, too, as she stubbornly followed the string of white stones. She had hoped to be through long before now.

Over one short passage the rock had been so hot the walls scorched her legs as High-Whisker raced through the dark, squealing in distress as his feet blistered. Three times they had lost the white stones under dust and rubble, wandering through side tunnels for what seemed like a year. In a few

63

places the fallen roof had half blocked the tunnel. High-Whisker bravely at her heels carrying her pack, she had climbed, wriggled, and squeezed between and under and over huge boulders.

Once, she had thought High-Whisker was jammed solid, that she would have to leave him there to die wretchedly behind her, but as she screamed and tugged at his whiskers and desperately dragged away stones, one of the leg-straps of his saddle had broken and he had managed to squirm through, scraped and cut by the rocks. She had sat trembling for a long time, hugging his neck with relief, till they both recovered enough to retrieve the saddle and go on.

Now, hand and footsore, covered in grazes and bruises, she stopped. The rough crack she was following had come to a junction, a cross-tunnel, lower, but smoother underfoot. Which way? She couldn't see the next stone. Wearily she peered away into the blackness on each side, but there was no clue. Behind her, High-Whisker sat down. Peepik was draped across her shoulder, asleep. What now?

It dawned on her slowly. This was the coal-mine! She'd done it!

Chooker celebrated with a sausage for herself and Peepik, a pie for High-Whisker, and a long drink for them all. She even took enough water to wash her face and bathe her sore hands and High-Whisker's paws, before treating her cuts—and his—with her germ-kill gelstick. He drank until the watersack was almost half empty, but he deserved it.

Screwing up her face, she pictured the map. Left? Yes, left. She pushed herself to her feet, rubbed High-Whisker's nose, scratched his ears, and told him, *Not far now, loyal friend!*

Round two corners, though, she came to a sharp right curve, that led round—and round—and round—and there was the tunnel she had come in by. This was a loop. A loop? Eh, she was recalling the map upside down! Yes, she should have gone right. Silly dodo! Eh, well, it wasn't far back.

Trotting footsteps clopped towards her.

She froze, a hand on High-Whisker's neck to keep him quiet, covering her lantern.

A faint glow approached round the corner, and she saw what she should have realized already, that in the dust the marks of her feet and the rat's claws were clear. *Back!* She shrank back out of sight—and the footsteps followed her tracks away round the circle.

As soon as the glow faded, Chooker crept forward. Yes, there were the prints of boots. These would lead back to the central mines! She climbed to lie flat along High-Whisker's back with the sagging watersack behind her. *Let's go!* she told him excitedly. Roused by her fresh energy he did his best, scampering along the passage while she clung to his neck, her head low beside his, holding out the lamp to light their way. Peepik clung to her shoulder, squeaking in excitement—well, he'd been carried all the way.

Behind them there was a shout of annoyance. But they were away!

It wasn't hard to follow the tracks. There were few side tunnels along here, and she had an idea of which way to go. The fast rat scurry left her pursuer well behind. Ten minutes' trot, and the path seemed familiar. Up and across here—and yes, here was the hole; success so far!

High-Whisker had carried her well, but Outside the cold would kill him. She had to leave him. Chooker dismounted and hugged his neck. *Eh, you pride of the rat pack! The finest, strong and clever and brave and kindly! A Coal will come here soon. Go back with her, and you'll be King of the whole farm in another year or two! I love you, I always will, you're wonderful!* He sniffed at her face, pleased by the praise but unhappy to part from her.

At last, she reluctantly pushed his nose aside, slipped her head through the carrying strap of her pack, tied the food bundle to it, lifted the watersack and slid down into the opening. She remembered how she had sensed Mungith through here, as clearly as if he was here now. She reached up to set her lamp on the edge of the hole and get a good hand-hold—

Someone gripped her wrist, and hauled her up into a light, towards a contorted monster's face, lit from below, its mouth open—

No! She screamed and flailed wildly. Peepik tumbled from her shoulder with a squeal of alarm, echoed by a grunt of annoyance from above, and she half-fell. As her feet scrabbled solid ground again she heaved herself up to the hand holding her and bit it.

The figure squawked and let go. 'Yow! You stupid cavy! Cheeky, big-headed runt!'

Chooker dropped to the broken, fallen rock, scrambling to escape, ignoring the sharp edges hurting her damaged hands, knees, and toes. Something snagged her ankle, dragged her back, she kicked—and then it sank in. 'Mungith. It's Mungith. Isn't it?' Her voice rose from a breathless, gasping whisper to piercing shrillness.

'Yes, you ninny! You've bitten half through my finger, you wild rat—'

'You're lucky!' Chooker shrieked. 'I'd have stabbed you if I could! Burn you, you great clumsy bullying moron!'

'Useless runt of a sea-squirt!'

'You dull!'

'Limpet-brain!'

'You second-rate louse on a cod's belly!'

'Rock-head! You useless chunk of clinker!'

'Guano-guts! You terrified me!'

'Serve you right, you three-legged spider crab!'

'You nearly scared me crazy!'

'Waste of time! You're crazy already!' At last his yelling bore down her screeches. 'What in the sight of the Little Gods do you think you're doing here? Trying to bring in the

Giants? How dare you? When the Council said no! You're big-headed as a dodo-cock, you think that you don't have to obey Custom the way all the rest of us do! I won't let you destroy the world—'

By this time, Chooker had got her breath back. She curled up near the top of the pile of rock nursing Peepik, who was cowering in her lap away from the shouting, and in furious frustration watched Mungith raging. Could she argue him out of it? No. Not the way he felt about the Giant, burn him! She couldn't get up, he was standing almost on her feet, he'd just grab her again.

Below him claws ticked lightly over the rock. A pointed, intelligent face loomed out of the darkness into the light of Mungith's glow-tube. High-Whisker come to help. He couldn't, of course. Wild rats might attack people, but tame ones were strictly trained not to bite . . . never . . . he wasn't going to . . . he couldn't . . .

He could.

Chooker set Peepik on her shoulder pad and sat watching, her mouth slightly open in disbelief, as the big rat looked up at the young man leaning over her waving his fist, hesitated, decided to do something about it, and almost apologetically bit Mungith's calf.

Time to go.

Her pack and bundle were still slung across her chest. She was up the broken scree into the ancient tunnel above and away while Mungith was still yelling.

The dust had long ago settled and the slow-growing algae had re-established a faint orange light. She could see quite well. But which way led Outside? Bastiyyal, guide me! Right? Right!

She turned left, and ran.

Below her, Mungith drove off the rat without difficulty. 'Get away, you crazy cavy—get off—leave me alone!' Guilty at breaking the first rule of proper behaviour, High-

Whisker backed away, squeaking apologetically. Mungith felt his calf. Only dents, not punctures—the stupid beast had that much sense. Where was Chooker?

He scrambled up the rubble and looked round. Which way? There, fresh scuff-marks on the ground! This tunnel was higher than the ones below. Even tall Mungith could easily run along it. Cursing his little cousin for a cross-eyed sea anemone, he raced off left.

As soon as he was out of sight round the first bend, Chooker crawled out of the crack she had hidden in and started to run in the opposite direction as silently as she could.

Something about the floor of the tunnel caught her eye, even as she belted along. Marks here and there, reddish blotches, as if something had disturbed the algae a while ago—the Giant's footprints! This was the right way!

Six sixty-steps down the tunnel, a scutter of claws behind her made her look back. High-Whisker was following her again.

You mustn't! Go back! But he trotted behind her, watching her mournfully, his nose whiffling hopefully until she relented. She knew she shouldn't, but it was so good to have company! Besides, Mungith would soon realize he was going the wrong way—there was the sound of his boots already, pelting towards her. *Eh, all right! Good fellow! Come here!* She swung on to High-Whisker's back and urged him into a flat run—

Behind her, there was a crash and clatter, the sound of a bad fall. A sudden silence.

She pulled up, hesitating. Was Mungith trying to trick her? She thought towards him; no, he was hurt, really hurt.

In an agony of frustration, she pounded High-Whisker's neck till he bucked in complaint. She couldn't leave Mungith, not hurt, where there could be wild rats around. But she couldn't stay, either. She must go on—she must!

8

Mungith was about four sixty-paces from the place where the floor had fallen, lying with his head against a rock. He must have tripped and knocked himself out. Why had the idiot taken off his helmet? Chooker got out her worn gelstick, and rubbed the stub on the bleeding bump to stop the blood and kill any germs. Yes, she was soft and stupid, but she couldn't leave him. She rolled him on to his side, just as he moaned.

When he opened his eyes properly, the first thing he saw was Chooker's glowering face. 'You bone-head!' she snarled.

'Bone-head?' It was the best thing she could have said; sympathy would have made him collapse. In a temper, he fought the pounding pain and dizziness. 'It was your rat's fault! I tripped, and couldn't get the sore leg under me fast enough.'

'Only bone-heads make a habit of getting hurt in mines!' Chooker huffed in annoyance. But she had to do what she could. 'Can you sit up?' She reached to help him.

He snatched at her wrist—and stopped with a gasp. She had been half expecting it, and out of his sight behind her leg her other hand had been holding her knife ready. Sullenly he let her twist her wrist free.

'Rotten kelp-stem! I thought you wanted me to help you!'

He glared at her, wincing as he settled back. The jerk had hurt his head all over again. 'I can't let you go! Not to get the Giants! You don't know what you're doing!'

'Yes I do!' She knelt out of reach and glared right back. But anger wouldn't help. 'Mungith, I'm not daft. I have thought about it. Really I have, over and over, Bastiyyal

69

witness my word. I must go. And you're not going to stop me. Now, do you want me to help you or not?'

Only a Wilder would call the Gods to witness a lie. Impressed despite himself by the gravity of her oath, Mungith shrugged a sullen shoulder. 'I suppose so.'

'Give me your word you won't try to grab me again, then!'

'Eh, all right!' But she waited for him to say it. 'I promise! Beliyyak witness my word!'

Nodding, Chooker sheathed her knife and leaned forward again. Carefully, she helped him push himself up until he could sit leaning against the wall.

Mungith slowly relaxed his clenched jaw and tried to smile. 'At least you didn't say, "This won't hurt." '

'Huh!' she snorted. 'If you can make jokes, you're not too bad. I'll see if I can call Distom.' She closed her eyes and composed her mind to think out towards her half-brother. *Distom! Distom, can you hear me? Mungith's hurt. Send help. Distom!* But it was a long way, and she was tired. Tired? Exhausted! And Distom wasn't well. She tried again and again, till she was sweating with the effort. Was there a flicker of answer, away out there? She opened her eyes, and shrugged. 'I don't know if he heard me. But he might have heard you already, when you fell. Anyway, who was it who was following me?'

'Eh, I'd forgotten about her. Giffaral. Coal.' Mungith smiled; he'd be glad of an Adult who knew what she was doing.

'I remember her.' Chooker smiled; she'd be glad of an Adult who knew what she was doing. 'She won't be long.'

Mungith licked his lips thirstily, and Chooker shook her head at herself. 'Eh, dodo-shells! I left the watersack behind. I'll go and get it. Don't go away!'

'Me?' Mungith snorted, heavily sarcastic. 'I think I'll start training for the Foundation Day races.' He eased his bottom, and winced; every twitch drove a knife into his head.

70

Chooker's pet was sniffing at the pack. 'Eh, leave that alone, you greedy rat!' Mungith hauled Peepik on to his knee and started to pet him.

High-Whisker was already lying down, licking his cuts and his sore feet to ease them. Chooker wished she could— she was filthy with coal-dust and she felt exhausted. She limped wearily along the passage.

As she reached the broken hole she jumped at the curses that blasted out at her. Giffaral had arrived.

It took a while to calm the angry Coal down enough to explain what had happened to Mungith, but at last Chooker managed it. To her surprise, Giffaral's temper vanished. 'Eh, clumsy chunk!' the Coal exclaimed. 'Men should stay out of mines. Trip over own feet like dodos. Bastiyyal favours women. Tougher, neater. More sense—wear helmets! I see to him. Often accidents in mines, no Silvers handy, eh?' Her confidence made Chooker feel much happier as she followed the stocky, muscular figure back up through the break and along the upper tunnel.

With firm, gentle fingers Giffaral felt Mungith's head. 'Can you move? Toes, fingers? Well.' She sat back. 'Skull not cracked, nor neck bones. Good solid rock head! Sore, eh?'

'Not too bad,' Mungith grunted. Everything was wavering; he felt sick, but he'd not admit it.

Knowing just how he felt, Giffaral grinned at him. 'Good lad! No fuss. Here.' She gave him a pain stop pill from her pouch. He puffed in relief as the pain faded. She scowled at him. 'Keep helmet on next time, eh?'

Then the Coal turned to study Chooker. 'What now?'

'I'm going on.'

'No, she isn't!' With the back-up, and the easing of his pain, Mungith's determination to stop his cousin had revived. 'She's crazy! She's going to get the Giants, stupid dodo! You've got to stop her, Giffaral!'

71

Giffaral shrugged. 'How? She can run faster than me.'

Chooker nodded in satisfaction. She had carefully placed herself on the outside of the group, just in case. 'You go for help, Giffaral. I'll stay with Mungith in case of rats.'

'Stay here?'

'Until somebody comes. I need the rest anyway. But as soon as I hear people coming, I'm going on!'

Rather to Chooker's surprise, Giffaral didn't argue. Mungith did. He complained, argued, pleaded, commanded, all over again. But Chooker simply sat, radiating defiance. *No, I won't stay, and nobody's going to stop me!* Not now, when she was more than half-way there!

At last, Mungith sank into a silent sulk. Giffaral scratched her nose, leaving a faint orange line in the black dust. 'I met Giant, too,' she observed. 'Stupid, not bad. I think we should meet, too. Not best this way. Trouble, fuss for Point.' She shrugged. 'Too late to stop that. So don't waste it. Specially when I can't stop you.' She slapped Mungith's shoulder lightly. 'Cheer up! We don't fight children. If Giants are same, she'll do better than Adult.'

Mungith humphed and ostentatiously turned away from them. Giffaral shook her head at his back, and then nodded to Chooker. 'You got this far. Maybe Bastiyyal likes you. I go for help. Not long. You drink, eat, rest.' She handed over the bag of painstops. 'One more if he needs it, not more. You keep. Good luck. Little Gods watch over you, but not too closely!' She grinned at Chooker, and set off back along the tunnel.

Chooker started to grin, too. Support from a Coal, one of the most traditional-minded Houses! Whatever next?

Mungith was sulking, High-Whisker was sleeping. Chooker relaxed and took a drink of water.

The thud of Giffaral's boots, echoing round the bends of the passage, stopped.

Voices. Giffaral, and two or three others.

72

Chooker shoved back the stopper and stood up. 'Is that more Coals already?' They'd probably not agree.

Mungith incautiously turned his head. 'Ouch! Doesn't sound like it.' The voices were angry, and not coming nearer.

'Come out of your shell, have you?' Chooker asked sarcastically. He glowered at her. 'I'll go and see.' Going wide round him, just in case, she trotted along the twisting tunnel, her sandals silent in the dust.

As she crept closer the echoes stopped bouncing and distorting the words.

'You'll wreck mines! Lava sealed off in there! Set fire to coal seams!' Giffaral was shouting at a group of six or seven people by a built wall just this side of the break in the tunnel floor.

'Think I'm a fool?' Chooker knew that harsh voice. What was Hemminal doing up here? 'I checked,' the Kelp jeered. 'Remember Mylooj, here? She was Coal House. She knows the maps. The gusher here isn't lava, it's water. But it'll fill this end of the mines. Granite and Block Houses can wall off all the link tunnels before it floods the whole place.'

Peering round the rocks from about thirty paces away, Chooker could see the sturdy little Coal facing the intruders, all taller and heavier than she was. 'So why do it?'

Hemminal snorted. 'You want Giants dancing along here into the City? Pyroonak doesn't. Nor me, nor anybody with sense. So we're making sure it doesn't happen. Saving the City. Public-spirited, that's us.' The Wilders behind her chortled.

Giffaral was horrified. 'Breaking a mine?' It was the worst act she could think of. She stared at the renegade Coal in disgust. 'Knew you were coward, Mylooj. Why we threw you out. Not saboteur. Won't let you!'

'How are you going to stop us?'

'Have to kill me!'

Someone sniggered.

Incredulous, Giffaral stared at the callous faces round her. 'You would!'

'We will.' Hemminal nodded indifferently. 'You've seen too much.'

Chooker crouched, frozen. It only needed Giffaral to try to save herself by saying that she wasn't alone, that there was a witness, and the Wilders would be charging along the tunnel—and Mungith lying there, unable to move . . .

Giffaral didn't even glance behind her. 'Duel?'

'You do think I'm a fool! You'll die in the burst. Bad luck, eh?'

Giffaral glared up at Hemminal with sheer contempt. 'Not just killing. Murder. Seems to me, worst of Giant's ideas are here already. What if you're wrong? If it is lava? If it burns the coal seams, fires the City?'

'It won't. Even if it was lava, the seams round here are cleaned out. Not a working coal-face within twenty sixty-paces, and even liquid lava would set long before it got that far.' Sneering, Hemminal chuckled. 'But Pyroonak will puff it up, say it's a real disaster. Father Ice and a couple of Granites will help him—not lie, but, well, exaggerate, see? And then we'll get rid of that pest of a Queen.' She lifted a rock from the side of the tunnel. 'Your body'll help prove it.'

Somehow Chooker's brain was working, even if her muscles were rigid with horror. In a disaster the Queen had to give herself as a sacrifice to appease the Little Gods, as the old Queen had done to stop the floo. If Prentast could be convinced to offer herself, King Pyroonak would get rid of her opposition, and make sure somebody easily managed was picked as next Queen. And Hemminal would run Atlantis.

What could she do?

Nothing. Not now. They were between her and the City— and she couldn't leave Mungith anyway. Please, Bastiyyal, keep him quiet! To give him and Chooker a chance to escape, Giffaral was deliberately hiding their presence, a brave, wonderful gift. Chooker bit her wrist to stop herself yelling in rage and frustration. She couldn't do anything . . .

Distom! Distom, I need you! Emergency! Wake up! Distom! Anybody! Help! Screwing up her face in absolute concentration, she screamed mentally as hard as she could, till sweat ran down her forehead and spine, cold and clammy.

No answer.

Sudden yells made her open her eyes. Giffaral had snatched out her knife and attacked the Wilders with all the might of her powerful miner's muscles. They went down in a struggling heap.

Hemminal raised the rock and poised it above the writhing, kicking, grunting bodies . . .

Chooker hid her face with her hands. At the horrible thud, her heart twisted till she felt it stop, and then started again slowly, painfully.

There was a clatter. 'That's that.' Hemminal had tossed the stone aside, and now kicked her friends to their feet. 'Eh, let's get a move on! Joossack's done for—that's another body.' Her voice was quite unmoved by the death of one of her friends. 'But there's nobody else wounded to death, so earn your pay, move, you dulls! Yarron, Frippig, drag Joossack and the Coal off to where they'll be found after the flood. The rest of you hit those chisels! That stone's soft enough to cut now.'

Kneeling frozen, Chooker suddenly recognized the stinging scent that had been twitching at the back of her nose; stone-melt. She peered round the corner. Hemminal's team began to chisel away the rock and ancient cement of a wall that must have been built many cycles ago to seal off the gusher. Softened by the acrid fluid, great globs and chunks of sticky stone cracked and crunched down.

75

'Careful! Wait,' a Coal voice grunted. Mylooj was holding a listening tube to the wall, tapping it, listening to the echo. She stood back. 'About as far in again. Go wider.' Two skin sacks of the fluid were squirted across the wall, and the work went on.

Chooker was afraid she would sneeze at the sharp stink. Her mind was spinning like a kelp frond in a whirlpool. Giffaral lying there, so small . . . Think of something else. Anything else. That much stone-melt must have cost strings of teeth. But Hemminal was rich now. So was Mungith—

A high whistle, at the edge of hearing, began piercing their ears. 'Air venting. Back, run back!' Mylooj waved her mates away from the tiny jet of steam spurting between the stones.

By Chooker's foot, a small black shape suddenly squeaked. Peepik had come to see what she was doing. Chooker grabbed for him, but too late; the rat dodged her hand, running nosily on down the tunnel.

Hemminal was looking at the steam, but the movement drew her eyes. A wild rat, going to get boiled! She chuckled.

The whistle came down the scale to merely painful, then spluttered. 'Come away!' Mylooj screamed. They started to back off fast down the tunnel.

Peepik sat up, rat-style, to rub his ears, and the bright chevrons on his collar gleamed in the dim light.

Hemminal jerked to full attention. 'A collar—it's that Point brat's pet! She's there—she's along there!' She snatched for her knife.

Mylooj grabbed her arm. 'No time! Get back to boat! Burst will kill! Run now!' Her tug delayed Hemminal for just a second before she was thrown aside as the Kelp swung forward—and stopped dead.

In that second, as Chooker watched, petrified, the softened wall of the tunnel burst open. Boiling liquid gushed out, a spurting torrent that splashed and splattered and poured both ways along the passage in a blinding, roaring fog of steam, cutting her off from the Wilders—and from home.

As Chooker fled up the tunnel, screaming in terror, drops scalded her legs, spurring her faster. She had to get Mungith away safe!

Something was missing. Where was Peepik?

He wasn't scampering at Chooker's heels. He was gone.

9

The rats had heard the whistle of escaping air several seconds before Mungith did. High-Whisker scrambled to his feet, shaking his head uneasily. Peepik trotted off to investigate.

Alerted by the movement, Mungith pushed himself up. His head was almost clear now. As High-Whisker started to back away along the tunnel, Mungith grabbed his whiskers to hold him back. What was wrong? What was that noise?

Squeaking with pain and fear, High-Whisker was tugging to escape. If the whiskers pulled right out and the rat ran off, Mungith thought, Rat House would blame him for losing one of their mounts. He pulled himself to his feet to get a better grip. He couldn't think to mounts as Rat House did, but ordered firmly, 'Stand still! Stand!' High-Whisker still dragged away. Mungith grabbed an ear to twist the rat's neck round. That was better. Thank Beliyyak for the pain-stop pill!

Chooker's pack, with the food-bag tied to it, nearly tripped him. If he took it, she'd have to go home. Even she couldn't go on without it. He let go with one hand and lifted the strap over his head to lie beside the strap of his knife sheath—

A mind-splitting roar blasted down the tunnel. A burst!

High-Whisker reared and squealed. He couldn't escape, not with his head bent round. Mungith hauled grimly, nearly dragged off his feet. Where was Chooker?

She raced into view, already waving at him to mount, shoved him upwards as he tried to argue that she should ride. Before he was settled in the saddle High-Whisker was bolting off along the tunnel. Chooker snatched his tail to be dragged along faster than she could have run alone, her tattered cloak flying.

Boiling water and mud at their heels, the bellow of the outbreak stunning them, they charged across open spaces, scrambled over and under slipping rocks and squeezed through narrows. Three times they had to race desperately back from dead ends, hoping the flood hadn't caught up to trap them. Once a swirl of white broth gushed from a side tunnel, and they had to splash through the hot soup to a path up and away.

Slowly the roar died behind them as the tunnels sloped upwards. They had been well warned about how far a burst could squirt a flood, and kept going; twenty sixty-paces . . . thirty . . . forty . . . The pressure in their ears dropped. They could hear their steps again, echoing into the distance down openings and branches on both sides of the winding tunnel. High-Whisker's panic flight slowed to a run, to a trot, to a stumble. He stopped, sides heaving, head drooping.

After a minute Mungith slid gasping from High-Whisker's back and Chooker sank exhausted beside him.

They were in a clear, open cave with a comfortable floor of fine gravel. In a minute, when Chooker got her breath back, she'd tell Mungith what had happened. But she was so tired . . . It was a full tide and more since she had started out on her adventure, and she had scarcely stopped moving in all that time. And then this last terrified race . . . She relaxed and gratefully leaned against her big cousin. Yes, he was a stupid clumsy conceited big bully; but for the moment he felt strong, warm, and comforting.

After a while, Mungith forced himself to move. He was the Adult, he had to take charge. 'Right, what happened?' Silence. 'Chook?'

She was sound asleep, cuddled into his shoulder.

In the middle of his pain, weariness, and fear, in his anger and bitterness, the solid little lump of confidence felt rather good. Silly little dodo . . .

He listened. Behind them the tunnels boomed low and far-off. Nothing nearby, just the rat panting. He laid Chooker's head down, and leaned over to undo High-Whisker's girths. With a great whuff of relief, the rat rolled and squirmed to rub up his fur, filthy and sticky with sweat and grit under the saddle pad, and then curled down beside Chooker. He'd wake if the flood came near.

Mungith unslung the pack. Good thing he'd taken it. What was in it? Food. Warm clothes and a blanket. She had been quite sensible. It was freezing cold here. They must be high above the lava and hot springs, up near the ice. He tucked the blanket and a thick cloak round them both, stuffed the rest back into the pack and slipped it under Chooker's head as a pillow. The saddle made a rest for his own aching head. After a while, he slept too.

Chooker woke first. Eh, what aches—lumps in her hammock—a dim orange-pink glow, not Point gold—a rasping noise; High-Whisker curled cosily beside her snoring on one side, Mungith sprawling on the other. The mine. Hemminal. The flood. Giffaral. Peepik. Eh, poor Peepik! He shouldn't have come. And poor Giffaral.

Eh, why didn't the Gods watch, when you really needed them? Silly idea; they did what they pleased, not what suited you.

Although she didn't move, just lay staring at the roof, Mungith suddenly blinked once and woke up fast, as he had learned to do during the last year. 'Where . . . what . . . eh, I remember.' In spite of the disaster he somehow felt better, as if the panic flight had burned away some of his sour anger. He even smiled slightly at Chooker as he stretched. 'Beliyyak, I'm stiff! And my mouth feels like a Wilder's armpit. I need a drink.'

'We left the watersack behind.' Chooker sat up, rubbing

her sore feet, not looking at him, unable to respond to his tentative friendliness. Her tone was as dusty as her thoughts.

Mungith snorted. 'There's no shortage of water behind us!' He sat up. 'Burn it, that hurts—my neck's stiffer than a stalactite. And what a lump!' His fingers explored the swelling.

Chooker fumbled in her pouch for a pain-stop. He chewed it and managed to find enough spit to swallow while Chooker shivered and drew the blanket up round her again. Ice House often worked in freezing temperatures, but everyone else was more used to warmth. 'You brought the pack.' She tried to show pleasure. 'Thanks.' Her voice was thin.

At least she hadn't realized why he had lifted the pack. Mungith shivered too, and opened it. 'We must be a long way from the lava and home. You've warm clothes in here.'

Silently, she nodded. He hadn't asked, but she'd have offered to share anyway. It wasn't worth making a fuss about. Even if she had the energy.

Two pairs of bright woolly leggings covered Chooker's legs and Mungith's bare arms. Chooker belted her warm feathery hooded cloak over her leather tunic. Her thick tunic strained across Mungith's chest under his good kilt, with the leather jacket on top, and the remnants of her sealskin cloak made leg-wraps for him. Chooker found socks and mitts for both of them, and stuffed the blanket, the clogs, and the lantern back into the pack.

'Right.' Tying the last knot of his leggings, Mungith spoke decisively. He still staggered if he shook his head, but he could ride. 'Breakfast, and then we'll head back. We can find our way easily, there's our track on the floor, among the crumbs—' He stopped.

Crumbs?

In a corner, the kelp bag flapped open, torn and empty.

Wincing with his sore paws, High-Whisker was contentedly grooming his rounded belly.

'Crazy, greedy—!' Mungith actually reached for his knife.

'Don't!' Chooker was horrified. 'Don't be stupid! You know rats eat anything, anywhere. He didn't know it wasn't his dinner!'

'Eh, Beliyyak drown him!' Mungith snarled. But they'd need the half-witted animal to carry them back. Though he shoved the knife back into its sheath, his frustrated anger boiled up again. 'Don't call me stupid! We've no food, no water, and a flood of boiling water between us and home, right? We're in a real mess. I'm supposed to thank him, maybe? And you! You brought us here!'

Chooker's face flamed. 'I never asked you to follow me!'

'You think I'd be here on my own? So what happened back there? What did you do?'

'Me? Go swallow a stalactite! It was Hemminal did it, your precious Hemminal! And she killed Giffaral, and I couldn't do anything, I couldn't . . . I couldn't—' Chooker gulped, struggling for control to speak sensibly.

As the story unfolded rather jerkily, Mungith sat appalled. Hemminal? Tried to kill Chook? Deliberately opened a gusher with stone-melt? Killed Giffaral? Planned to destroy Prentastal? No. It wasn't true. Couldn't be. His face grew grimmer and grimmer. 'I don't believe a word of it. You've always hated Hemminal, you're jealous because I admire her!' He knew inside himself that he was whipping up his anger. He couldn't dismiss what Chooker said, not entirely. But he couldn't accept it, either. 'Maybe you misunderstood. Or you're making up stories!'

'I'm not a liar!' Chooker was outraged. 'I challenge you! How dare you say I'm a liar!'

He sneered down at her. 'Eh, don't be silly, I can't fight you!'

'Well, I can fight you!'

'Adults don't duel with children!' But he wasn't being quite fair. 'I never said you were lying. But you do exaggerate! You can't deny that!'

'Not this time! This isn't a game, whelk-brain!'

Mungith could see she was serious; but it couldn't be true . . . She wouldn't lie . . . But no, she must be wrong, of course she was! 'Anyway, we've got to get back. Even you can't go on now, not with no food! So come on. Maybe the flood's gone down, drained away into the main stream. We'll find a way back through the mines somewhere—they all link up. I'll take you back, if we have to walk half-way round the City to find it!' Mungith turned to lift the saddle and whistle High-Whisker. Wretched, and blaming Chooker for his misery, he scowled at her. 'And I'll see you're properly punished for this!'

Something seemed to snap in Chooker's chest. Mungith—her own big cousin—he hated her. He'd get her whipped, or outlawed to the Wilders' caves. Bastiyyal burn the stinking hagfish, he'd do anything rather than face the truth about Hemminal. He'd personally shove her out of Death Gate! To think she had planned to marry him! He preferred Hemminal. What a silly fool she had been, not to let herself realize it before! But she'd not let the lousy codfish beat her!

Silently, stealthily, she gripped her pack and crept off till she was well out of reach; turned and raced down the tunnel as fast as her aching legs and screaming feet would take her.

Mungith's bellow of fury echoed after her. 'Stop, Chooker! I'll have your hide for a pair of sandals! I'll get you!'

He wasn't well enough to run far and fast, so he still had to saddle High-Whisker. She whistled shrilly and called back, shouting and thinking, 'High-Whisker! Come here! Come to me! *Best of rats, leave him, come here!* Come on! *Break away, come to me, my champion!*'

While she wasn't touching the big rat, her thoughts were faint. High-Whisker tried to obey her words, but without much urgency, and Mungith had time to get a good grip of his whiskers. 'Eh, no way, rat!' he grunted. 'We're going after her all right, but I'll be on your back! Wait till I get these girths fastened! Stand! Stand still!'

Enough of what Mungith was saying and thinking got through to High-Whisker to make him obey his training. Twitching with eagerness, he stood still long enough for Mungith to tighten the straps round his front legs and tail, swing himself up and grip the pack-rings on the saddle. 'Right! Now you can go! I'm coming for you, Chooker!' he yelled in triumph.

Chooker wasn't very far ahead, retracing their tracks in the dust. He mustn't catch her!

A deep crack at the foot of one wall caught her eye. Deep enough to hide under? To her surprise, it opened up beyond into a cave. She squeezed through, and heard the patter of High-Whisker's claws run past. *That's right, keep going! Run as fast as you like!* she thought gleefully to him, and sensed his relief that at last both his people were telling him to do the same thing.

The light was so dim that even Chooker's sensitive eyes couldn't see where it was safe to put her feet. She had to pause to light her lantern.

There was only half a candle left, and no more in her pack—High-Whisker must have eaten the others. She bit at her knuckles in dismay. Should she go on?

What else? She'd not go back home, to humiliation and disgrace at best!

While she groped in her pouch for her little fire-jar, a faint red glow caught the corner of her eye. When she looked straight at it, it vanished, but when she looked aside again, yes, it was there. And another, further on. The Giant's footmarks again! This could be the way out—or, at least, Bil had come this way.

Or another Giant, maybe? Hunting for naughty children and lost miners, as the Nurses said . . .

Eh, nonsense! All it meant was that Giants had come here. So from here, there was a path to Outside; and if it was big enough for a Giant, it was big enough for her! This was what she had hoped for, wasn't it?

Wasn't it?

And if they did eat her, it was still better than going back.

Her heart thumping, Chooker uncapped her fire-jar and blew gently on the film of jelly inside till it flickered into a brief, frail flame, just enough to light her candle. She clipped the lid down, stowed it away, and held up the lantern. A natural crack, the floor silted up with gravel and sand, twisted out of sight. She stiffened her courage and went on.

Within two minutes Mungith realized she was no longer in front of him. Cursing her, he slapped High-Whisker's neck. 'Stop! Stop! Find Chooker! Go back, find Chooker! Turn round—that's right—now go back. Hunt her!' He'd catch her!

Enjoying the new game, High-Whisker trotted back and fore for a while, and at last found the crack. He sniffed at it eagerly. 'She went in here? Good rat!' Mungith slipped off to crawl through the low opening. 'I'll catch her! Ow, my head! Beliyyak drown the little fool! Come on, squeeze under, there's room to ride inside here.' He shook his glow-tube to stir up the light, clambered back on to High-Whisker's saddle, and urged him, 'On! Go on! Find her! I'll get her!'

Several times Mungith had to dismount, to squeeze past or duck under jutting rocks, but High-Whisker scuttled on confidently; Chooker was still ahead. The pain-stop pill was wearing off. Mungith winced and grunted as every twitch of his head jarred his neck. At each jab of agony his temper grew redder. How dare Chooker do this to him?

The crack suddenly opened out into a high cave, and there she was. 'Got you!'

Chooker was clambering up a steep scree leading up the far wall. At his triumphant yell, she glanced back. 'Go away! Leave me alone!' He'd drawn his knife! What under the roof was he playing at? She turned to flee up the slope. The stones rolled under her driving feet and threw her back down, to sprawl sobbing with the pain of her grazes and fear of her cousin's anger. 'No! No!'

In triumph, Mungith brandished his knife. The hunt was over. He'd won! He'd stop her! He'd get her! He slapped his mount with the flat of the long blade to drive him forward.

High-Whisker had never been struck in his life. He put down his head and bucked.

Mungith was jolted and heaved around the cave, screaming with pain and rage, holding on frantically with one hand, the knife waving wildly in the other. He'd stab himself if he wasn't careful—

From the hole above slashed a beam of light, a blinding brilliance. A huge howling figure launched itself down the scree in a roar of sliding stones.

Mungith, already unsteady, lost his grip altogether and was tossed. Squealing in terror, High-Whisker fled off down the tunnel.

Too scared to move, Chooker stared at the figure clambering to its feet beside her knees. She knew the light—it was a tawch, like the one Bil had had. But the monster holding it was round and puffy-fat, its skin shiny red and silver, and its eyes! It had four eyes, huge and round and flat, not human at all.

Another light flared. A second Giant, even bigger, all yellow and black, with two ordinary eyes and two flat ones, appeared at the top of the slope.

Scrambling to his feet, hunting his fallen knife, Mungith was sobbing in pain and fury. He'd stop her—she mustn't talk to the Giants—they might hurt her—she'd destroy Atlantis—got the knife—he'd save her! Knife in fist he swung round and dived towards her.

The yellow Giant at the top of the slope screamed, and he glanced up.

A stone rolled under his foot. He staggered. The Giant beside Chooker yelped as the blade ripped through its red skin, and hit at him hard.

Its hand hit Mungith's chest, and knocked him right off his feet. For the second time in a day, his head hit a rock. Bonelessly Mungith melted into the pile of stones.

10

Mungith moaned. Eh, his head was splintering . . . dazzling . . . something over his eyes. He pawed feebly at the irritation. A sharp, sweetish, unnatural smell. Very dry air.

'Mungithak?' A huge blurred figure all in white leaned over him, patted his arm gently, and bobbed its head forwards, the way Bil had nodded. A Giant. 'Okay, Mungithak, okay,' it murmured. He lay still, too terrified to move. It smiled at him—in triumph?—its teeth white in bright pink lips, its skin and breath stinking of unknown foods, and moved away without hurting him.

His neck was held tight in a wide, stiff padded collar. He felt sore and bruised all over. The things over his eyes were lenses of darkish hard-gel, held by a stretchy strap behind his head. No, he shouldn't move them, he'd be blinded by the room's brilliance. He was lying on a softish platform, long and wide, with a cover over him.

He gasped at a touch on his arm. Two heads loomed by his shoulder. One was a small Giant, the other much lower. He struggled to focus on them. They both had glass eyes— no, lenses; the Giant's were clear, the little one's black. It had long black hair, too, and a red tunic. Chooker. He wasn't alone among enemies. 'Chooker—you're safe!' Incredibly relieved, he pushed himself up, ignoring the pounding of his head, and reached out a hand. For some reason she flinched away. 'Where are we?'

'A Giant House. They carried you here in a land-boat, a big box with skids and wheelses, just like Bil said, and looked after you.'

'Can you talk to them? Sense them?'

She shook her head. 'But hands and acting can say a lot.'

The Giants moved restlessly. Chooker smiled up. 'This—' she gestured to the taller one in the white tunic—'this is Annabel.' Annabel bobbed its head, smiling. 'Annabel's a woman Giant.' Mungith felt astonished—and then silly. Of course there must be women Giants. 'And this one's a boy. Peter.'

'Hi, Mungithak!' the Peter Giant squawked. 'Sawree!'

'That means he's apologizing. He's the one who hit you, to stop you killing him—or me.' Chooker's tone was grim.

'Chooker! I wanted to save you!'

Chooker's distrustful face didn't change. 'You had your knife out before the Giants came.'

Hot shame scalded Mungith. 'No . . . no!' But it was true. How could he have done that to Chook? He'd been a total idiot.

He lay back, groaning. Chooker's lips tightened, but she fished out another pain-stop for him, and the Annabel Giant offered him a glass cup of fizzing water. Poison? It—she—studied his suspicious expression, grinned and took a mouthful itself. Herself. 'Okay!' Mungith sipped gingerly; the water had a sweetish, tangy taste that freshened his mouth and settled his stomach. She stood back, smiling and nodding forward. 'Okay, Mungithak.' 'Okay' must mean 'good'.

He had been washed and cared for. He was wearing loose leg-warmers, joined at the top, and a thin tunic that tied at the front with flat knobs through slits. They'd not have dressed him if they were going to cook him. Surely?

Something knocked. Annabel opened a door and took in a tray. Peter beckoned Mungith and Chooker. 'K'mawn! Grubsup! Food, okay? Yookan situp? Okay!'

While Peter set out food on a table, Annabel helped Mungith sit up against the pillows and laid the tray on his knees. Chooker needed two cushions on her chair. Mungith blinked at it. No, his eyes weren't that blurred. It had four legs instead of three. The floors here must be very flat.

The food was stuff like red and green kelp stem, crunchy fried fingers of something white inside a brown skin, and cod in a white sauce. It all tasted odd and dull, but Chooker was starving, even if Mungith felt too sick to eat much. Annabel and Peter used a queer spiky tool, but after exchanging glances Chooker and Mungith stuck to the normal knife, spoon, and fingers. Then there was an iced cream with some sweet yellow chunks. And that was that. Chooker sighed for the loaded table at home. But maybe Giants were poor, like Roof Families. It wouldn't be Manners to ask for more.

All through the meal, Peter kept on talking and polishing his lenses. He told them words; 'Chipz—eet—drink—in—awn—head—sore—noh—glassez—bed—hawt—cohld. My hand—yoor hand—hur hand—hiz hand.' Peter didn't seem to be able to say the Atlantan words and seemed surprised that they could remember the silly short Giant words so easily. Giants used lots of little words in an odd order. 'Yoo giv plate too Annabel. Ie siddown awn chair; Annabel getup. Shee pickup camcorder. Ie hav sore hand.' He showed them his right hand, tightly bandaged.

Annabel spoke into a bone thing on the wall, and soon Giants began to arrive. They were clearly trying to be calm, but they were so excited that they couldn't help staring at the youngsters, talking louder and faster, waving hands, arguing and interrupting each other with no Manners at all. 'Wair . . . How . . . Wot . . . Wy . . . ?' they demanded of Annabel, who kept shrugging helplessly and obviously explaining over and over just how they had all met.

'Like the Council!' Chooker commented, perched uneasily on the bed beside her cousin.

Mungith winked at her. He was feeling better, more relaxed, in spite of his uncomfortable collar and silly clothes. The City had been curious about the Giant. This was just the same.

Chooker tried to keep calm to study the dozen or so Giants studying them.

All the Giants had small eyes, some, like Peter, with lenses over them. Most had brownish hair, cut short rather like Hunters. Two had darker skins and hair. Three had beards. Some were probably women. Some were taller, some fatter, but all were the same basic pattern, dressed in thick woolly tubes, and all enormous. Chooker felt overwhelmed. She was glad of her knife, hanging handy round her neck.

Last of all, the King arrived, the one everyone stopped talking for. Chooker rose to bow politely.

King Doctormurry was rather older than the rest, with a dark, pointed beard. He barked questions, snorting in hostile disbelief at Annabel's answers, sneering at the youngsters. Annabel pointed out Chooker's tunic and sandals, showed him her feather cloak and clogs and Mungith's glowtube and—to his relief—his knife, in its sealskin sheath. The King grunted contemptuous dismissal of it all, till with a sudden 'Hey?' he snatched at Chooker's hand, peering rudely at the fifth finger.

She winced. Crackling through his skin she could sense a kind of nervous anger. Maybe she could touch his mind . . . She jerked away with a cry of disgust.

'What's wrong?' Mungith demanded protectively.

'I tried to sense him, and he's horrible! Ready to snap like a mother cavy!'

King Doctormurry bent down to Mungith. 'Wair . . . yoo . . . from!' he said. Mungith blinked at him. The Giant repeated it, louder, almost shouting.

Peter slipped in between them, looking peeved. 'Heer . . . thair.' His hands showed what he meant. 'Yoo kum heer. Heer iz scotbais. Thair iz?' He pointed to 'thair', outside the house, and looked a question. 'Heer iz scotbais. Thair iz?'

91

Gently, Chooker touched his wrist. She was almost sure she knew what was being asked . . . yes. She beamed at him. 'Atlantis,' she said. 'Thair iz Atlantis.'

'Atlantis?' Annabel gasped. She said it wrong, but she clearly knew the name.

'Atlantis,' Mungith repeated, stressing the 'At' to correct her.

Startled, the Giants stared at them. 'Atlantis?' they repeated, louder and louder.

'Heh! Rubbish!' Doctormurry snarled in a loud, hectoring voice. An awkward silence fell. 'Rubbish!'

Mungith stiffened; did they think he was lying? He reached for his knife.

Doubtfully, Annabel held it away, looking at Chooker. 'Giv? Ie giv nife too Mungithak?'

Scarlet with shame, Mungith had to wait for his little cousin to consider him carefully—but maybe he couldn't blame her. With a disturbing mixture of gratitude and resentment, he took the knife and sheath as they were handed to him at her nod, and felt a huge relief as he slipped the belt over his head and settled it on his shoulder. 'Okay! Thankyoo!' He sighed with satisfaction at being able to defend himself, as the Giants clapped and smiled.

Chooker was still watching him warily. 'I'm not going to go crazy with it!' he assured her. 'You can trust me—yes, I promise you can! Beliyyak witness my word!'

Chooker sniffed, but relaxed. No, he wouldn't go for her, not now. But how could they make King Doctormurry believe them?

Peter winked to her, and slipped through the crowd to the door. Suddenly, the light stopped. Everyone jumped, exclaimed—and gasped. In the dark, the glow-tube and Mungith and Chooker's skins shone gently. 'See!' Peter crowed. 'Itz troo! Didjeversee thatbifore? See! Notrix! Sowhynot Atlantis?' He started the light again, babbling twenty to the dozen, jumping up and down in shockingly bad-Mannered triumph until Annabel told him firmly to settle down.

All the Giants were talking at once, re-examining the glow-tube and knife. Peter gestured to Chooker and Mungith to take off the eating knives hung round their necks and remove the protective strip of hard-gel clipped round the half-circle blades. He pointed out to everyone the glass edge bonded along the bronze. 'It noh braik, braik, braik?' he asked.

Chooker showed them how tough and sharp the lava glass was. Mungith's was very thin now, down to two layers, but Chooker was more careful. Even after five years of use hers still had fourteen layers left of the original sixteen. However, since the outer layer was rather chipped, she tapped it off to show the Giants how to make a fresh edge. It seemed to astonish them.

When King Doctormurry took out a small box of white stems and tried to light one with a fire-box which just made sparks, Chooker fished out her own fire-jar and politely offered him the little blue flame. He blinked in astonishment. The smoke smelt dirty and sharp, like a cross between nose-clear resin and stone-melt. It must be medicinal, she thought, good for the lungs—well, you wouldn't breathe that stink for pleasure.

'He's more impressed by that than by my knife!' Mungith commented. 'Dodos! What else have we got?' Grinning, he emptied from his pouch a coil of hair twine and three fish-hooks, his note-pad, two silver needles but no thread in a hollow bone tube, two rings, a little black glass mirror, a silver ring with his ivory nailfile, ear scoop, tweezers, and toothpick clipped to it, a stick of perfume, a tassel of seal teeth and some odd ones. Chooker's pouch held the little bag of pain-stops—when she gave Mungith another, a Giant begged for one and seemed delighted; her own sewing set with twists of four types of thread, a hair tie, her child's help-call whistle, her gelstick, a magnifying lens, three loose rat teeth, a comb, a torn-off saddle buckle, most bits of a carved bone puzzle, and at the bottom, rather to her embarrassment, two pink spicejellies covered in fluff.

Each of them, of course, had their soul-stones. Chooker's, on the left of her nose because she was female, was a feather carved on a seal tooth, that had last been worn by a Granite, and Mungith's was an irregular red pearl that was once worn by a Queen. Chooker wondered if she should try to describe how when a baby left his parents' bed to go into the Nursery, his nose was pierced and the Priest gave him a soul-stone. Now he was a real person. When he died the stone would be returned to the big crystal bowl in the Royal House. No; she didn't think she could explain that.

The Giants were fascinated by it all.

Chooker and Mungith found they could understand Peter better than any of the other Giants. He acted the questions more vigorously, and he seemed to understand them, too. Chooker thought he was sensing slightly. After a while, he was translating all the Giants' questions and answers.

Yes, Atlantis was under stone and ice, in caves.

How many people? Mungith shrugged. It varied between one and two sixty-sixties, but was less now, after the floo. Anyway, nobody knew exactly. The Priest could judge roughly, by the number of soul-stones left in the bowl; when the level fell too low, the Mothers stepped up their birth control.

How far? Chooker shrugged. Distance depended on your load, how many dolphins and paddlers your boat had and which way the tide was running, or the strength of your rat and the smoothness of the path. Many steps away? Yes, many steps.

'Yoo kidz, like mee?'

'Noh, ie like—' Mungith pointed to one of the older Giants, and bristled as they grinned. 'Man? Okay, man. In Atlantis, Distomak heer, Prentastal heer.' Mungith indicated Distom's height, smaller than Chooker, and Prentast's, a hand taller than himself, just shorter than Peter.

'Pigmiz,' someone commented. Annabel frowned.

Then Peter asked, 'Unkelbil . . . er . . . Bil? Yoo see Bil?' The King Giant tensed.

Mungith looked at Chooker for help. He really didn't want to talk about this.

'Bilwinstonbil,' she said. All around eyes blinked, heads nodded.

'Bil Winston,' Peter said. He pointed to himself. 'Peter Winston.'

Annabel copied the motion. 'Annabel Winston.'

Chooker swallowed. Winston must be Bil's House, and Annabel and Peter were members of it. Eh, well. She had to tell them. She took Peter's hand and called her mind firmly to calm. The otherness of the Giant mind made her stomach squirm, but she could bear it. Maybe because Peter was a boy, it wasn't as strange as Bil's mind had been. She sent the image—*the mine, the fall* . . .

Mungith tried to say it in the words he had learned. 'Bil kum in Atlantis, in cave,' he said, while Chooker tried to think it to Peter. The young Giant suddenly blinked and jumped; the frail link was broken by his astonishment. He stared round, saying something in a dazed voice. The other Giants all looked astonished. King Doctormurry snorted.

'Bil woz in Atlantis?' Annabel asked. 'Hee dident kum owt with yoo? Wynot?'

Peter bit his lip, trying to sort out his thoughts. 'Cave fell?' Peter said, slowly, as if he didn't believe it. He shook Chooker's arm. 'Ded?' He mimed collapsing, his head flopping. 'Bilzded?'

Slowly, reluctantly, Chooker nodded. 'Bilzded.'

Slowly, sadly, unsurprised, Peter nodded. Annabel looked stunned. Peter put an arm round her shoulders. They were both sorrowful but not crying. It had been a year, after all. Everybody was silent, even the King.

'Annabel and Peter are Bil's Family,' Chooker whispered.

Absently Mungith nodded; he had already realized that. What would the Giants do? Would they want a duel to avenge Bil? Or didn't Giants duel? Would they just attack? His hand was ready to snatch out his knife . . .

Suddenly Annabel clapped her hands to snap herself out of her sadness and interrupt the meeting. 'Itslait. Bedtime!' she declared, and started to chase out the other Giants, repeating, 'Timorra!' when they tried to stay. At last, clearly against his will, King Doctormurry nodded a brusque agreement. He nodded down at Chooker and Mungith with an attempt at a smile, and marched out with the rest, their voices loud in argument and comment as they went off.

Peter was still looking dazed. He touched his forehead again, and pointed to Chooker's head. 'Yoo tawk too mee? In my hed?' When Chooker nodded, the boy Giant started muttering to himself in disbelief, but his face showed a dawning delight.

'K'mawn, Peter!' Annabel and Peter helped Mungith to walk down a high tunnel to another room with two huge soft beds in it, sat him down on one, pulled thick curtains to keep out the light from Outside, patted the other bed, and told Chooker, 'Sleep.' She mimed putting her head down on her hands and closing her eyes.

'Sleep? It's not all that long since we slept in the caves,' Chooker muttered. But all the excitement had exhausted her, and Mungith was looking very pale.

In a bathroom next door Peter opened a shower of hot water for washing. He seemed surprised that it didn't surprise them; didn't he think real people had bathrooms?

'I wonder how that wheels spout works,' Mungith commented. 'Good trade item.'

'So's this mirror. The glass must stop the silver tarnishing. And this frothy gel cleans dirt off well. We'll find out how they're made and make our fortunes when we get back.'

When they got back . . .

In silence, Mungith climbed wearily on to the bed. When they got back, he'd have to see she was punished. Somehow, it seemed less urgent. Less right.

'Goodnite,' Annabel and Peter murmured at the door.

'Goodnite,' Chooker repeated politely. It must mean 'sleep well' or something like that. The door closed.

Chooker sighed. Mungith was already asleep. Funny, that he seemed to trust Giants more than she did, now. Maybe it was the bump on the head.

She slipped the itchy lenses off her eyes. That was more comfortable.

Well, so far so good. She had found the Giants, and they were good people—well, most of the ones she had met. That hostility in the King . . . Distom would be able to explain it.

Eh! She had forgotten about Prentast! Bastiyyal, what should she do?

In spite of her jump of alarm, she yawned. So much had happened—but it wasn't her fault . . .

Think about it tomor—

11

Next day Mungith's head no longer felt as if it would fall off if he moved it.

Breakfast was boiled eggs, too small for dodo, the wrong shape for cormorant, but recognizable. He had three, in a huge Hall, with a dozen Giants in the House at tables all round, trying not to stare. It was quite enjoyable, even though he looked a mess, with bruises and scrapes all over, this stupid white collar they insisted he must wear, two bumps on his head like a dolphin, and these dark lenses over his eyes. At least his short Hunter haircut was neat, and he had his good black sealskin kilt, the dust polished off the embroidered bronze chevrons so that they gleamed. The Annabel Giant had offered him a 'teeshirt', but this House was so warm he didn't need a top, and he wanted his tattoo to show.

Chooker picked at an egg with her eyes down. What should she do? She couldn't concentrate on the new words Peter was babbling at them.

To his satisfaction, Mungith realized that he was learning better than Chooker. Well, he thought kindly, she was just a child, even if she was a Senser. Soon, he was talking to the Giants round about, who were grinning, encouraging and applauding him. Giants obviously weren't all bad—well, he'd known that, of course, he'd just been properly wary. It wouldn't do to tell Chooker she was right, though, her hair would puff like yeast buns.

When they were finished Peter led them on a tour of the House. In spite of the dark lenses, their eyes were soon sore from the brilliance through the windows. Outside, the pale blue roof was incredibly high and far away, and the blazing light of the Great God Rassiyyak glinted and reflected all round off blue-white ice and a wide blue-black sea to dazzle them.

Chooker had seen it the day before, briefly, as Annabel had carried Mungith out of the caves. However, she had been far too terrified to take much notice of her surroundings, hand over her eyes, huddling her head down into her cloak to escape the dreadful glare, forcing herself to clamber with the Giants over the ice and into the smelly alien boat, and hold Mungith steady as it crunched down the hillside. Now, when Peter opened a door for them, she shrank back and grabbed Mungith's arm. 'Noh, noh! I noh goh owt!'

Mungithak was willing to go out, but he felt he couldn't insist. He tugged Chooker's plait gently. 'Okay, we'll stay inside.' For now; but he'd adventure Outside as soon as he could.

Everywhere were new marvels. Chooker hadn't realized Giants would be so overwhelming, or that their Houses would be so vast and bright and cornery, not like the worn, cosy curves and hollows at home. The floors were dreadfully flat and hard on the feet in spite of the furry covers here and there. The smells were not the familiar, warm scents of many people and seaweed and yeasts, but stinging to the nose. All the Giants beamed down at them, raised a hand and said 'Hi!' in a friendly way. Chooker never once felt threatened, but nothing was natural. It was all far stranger than she had ever imagined. Too strange. Mungith strode along confidently, oddly seeming happier than she was. But then, he was a good deal taller, almost shoulder-height on some of the smaller Giants.

At last they came to a new room, where Annabel was waiting. 'Hi, Chooker, Mungith! Sleep good? Okay! Siddown heer.' She made a glass window on a big box light up, with blobs of bright colour moving inside. Mungith and

Chooker stared blankly at it. Peter's face lost its smile. He pointed at the box. 'Teevee! Viddy-oh! Thatz yoo!' he proclaimed. 'Look—thatz Mungithak, thatz Chooker, thatz mee! Wee filmd yoo awn the camcorder!'

They gazed again at the box—and jumped, startled. As Peter pointed, a face suddenly grew out of the colours under his hand. Chooker's face, just like in the mirror last night but small; the dark glassez over her eyes, her black plait, her mouth. Mungith chortled. 'Yes, I see it! Look, Chooker! There's your face in the—teevee?' Peter nodded, grinning.

Peter started the blobs moving again, and Mungith sat entranced. 'Thatz mee? Okay!' Yes, that was Chooker's voice, and Peter teaching them words. It was a copy of what had happened yesterday. Like remembering looking through a window. Enthralled, he stared into the teevee box. Clear and bright, wonderful! Eh, what a bump on his head!

Chooker's stomach churned. How had Annabel copied them inside that box?

Annabel sat by a table and opened a pad of white sheets. 'Want too see this? Itz a book.' Whatever it was, it would be less disturbing than looking into that teevee! Chooker scrambled to kneel on a chair. The book showed pictures of things Outside: Cities, Giants, wheels boats called car or bus or train depending on their size, birds and animals and fish. Giants seemed to like pictures. Some of them she knew— dolphins, seals. Annabel seemed astonished when she didn't recognize a thing like a cross between a bird and a seal, called a pengwin. Apparently huge crowds of them lived Outside. Chooker shrugged. They didn't come into the caves.

After a while, the teevee stopped. Rather disappointed that he couldn't watch himself any longer, Mungith joined them at the table. Annabel showed them another book, with more pictures. 'Heerz the wurld. Heerz antartica. Heerz scotbais. Okay? Heerz nyoo zeeland. Peter and mee, wee kum from nyoo zeeland, from sowth ieland, see heer? Kriest church, sowth ieland, nyoo zeeland.'

Chooker had her hand on Annabel's wrist to try to understand. 'Mungith, she's got everything inside out, like Bil. She thinks people live on the outside of a ball instead of the inside of a cave.'

'We'll be able to put them right soon, when we know more words.' He nodded kindly to the Giants.

After a while, Peter led them back to the Hall for slices of softish white stuff with cheese and meat and a spicy pickle in the middle. 'Okay!' Mungith approved. He and Chooker ate several, with a white drink. 'Is this milk? It's stronger than cavy milk,' he commented.

'Better add water to it. In case it gives us the squirts,' Chooker advised.

When they returned to the room, Mungith asked for the teevee again. Peter started it for him, and came to sit on a chair beside Chooker. He touched his head, grinning. 'Want to tawk in hed?'

Why not? Better than teevee. Chooker reached to take his hand.

Every time, the link came easier and the queer flavour of the Giant's mind upset her less. *Calm, don't strain, easy, open* . . . Peter accepted it naturally, as if he was used to calming his mind, which was odd because he wasn't a quiet boy. *Good tide, Peter—hi!*

Hi! It's working! Yayy! He made a triumphant face to Annabel, who gestured to him to go on. *Okay, okay! Hey, Chooker, can you show me your home?*

Chooker recalled the view of the whole City that she had seen—only what, sixteen, twenty tides ago?—sitting with Distom: *The circling terraces, the glowing colours.* Peter touched her arm, rubbed gently at the golden skin. *Yes, that's right, everything glows.*

She jumped; Annabel had taken Peter's other hand. Her mind was busy, jostling with other thoughts, irritating like something in your eye. Chooker almost broke the link, but Peter said something and Annabel gradually flattened her mind.

Chooker turned her thoughts home. *Distom, small and kindly; Mother.* Annabel laughed out loud as Chooker unconsciously started acting, mimicking Mother's dramatic poses while she was thinking about them. *Point House. The mosaic floors and arched ceilings, the well-stocked store-rooms, the bustling heat of the Kitchen, the subdued noise of lessons and work in the Hall while the off-tide slept in the dormitories, the Nursery play, the relaxed din at meals.* Peter was bubbling with glee beside her, his mind smoothly tucked into Chooker's, going with her like a young cousin she was showing round, enjoying, admiring, and appreciating. *Prentast's Wedding Feast. Prentast as Queen.*

'Teevee stop!' Mungith complained.

Annabel jumped, losing the link.

Prentast. Hemminal. I must save Prentast. I must go home! Mee too! thought Peter.

'Ile pootona nuther viddy-oh for Mungith,' Annabel said, and went over to press knobs on the teevee and start it again.

Chooker gaped at Peter. Did he really say—? Yes, he was grinning wide, nodding, as Annabel came back to the table.

This time Annabel didn't try to link, but spoke to Peter, who tried to send thoughts as she directed him. He pictured a series of scenes: *Bil going into a cave, with a bubble coming out of his head*—startled, Chooker nearly broke contact until she realized this was showing what Bil was thinking—*holding a scene of tiny people inside caves. Doctormurry shaking his head, saying, 'Noh, noh!' Bil in a cave. The same cave, empty—then filled with people searching, calling 'Bil, Bil!' Bil as Chooker had shown him the night before, lying hurt in the mine. Doctormurry smiling.*

102

Blinking with the effort of sorting all this out alone from the blurs, blinks, and shifts of Peter's untrained mind, Chooker thought to him what she had understood. *Bil said that people lived in the caves, and searched for them. Doctormurry said Bil was wrong. When he disappeared Doctormurry wasn't upset.* 'Okay?'

Pleased, although rather startled at the last bit which he had not meant to send, Peter puffed and nodded to Annabel. 'Shee gottit!' He started again. *I'm Bil's brother's son. Annabel is Bil's sister. She looks at*—something about holes in the roof, that Chooker didn't understand. *Annabel crying. She came to work here, to look for Bil in the caves. I came to visit her.* In the back of his mind, Chooker felt a swift jab of disappointment, linked with his hurt hand and—a Battle? He didn't want to come here; he had wanted to go to take part in some kind of fighting, but his mother had stopped it. She put it aside for now. *We went into the caves to look for him—and found you. Shock, cheers! Doctormurry is raging—he'll look a fool for sneering at Bil, when Bil was right.* That explained why Doctormurry was so hostile. Chooker smiled at Peter.

Annabel smiled, too. 'You wantoo try tawk too mee now? In hed?'

Chooker drew back. 'Noh. Hed sore.' It ached with the effort of making contact on her own with the alien minds, and Annabel would be much harder than Peter. She needed a rest. Shaking her head at Annabel, she slid down from the chair and went out.

Peter looked round. Mungith was happily watching a children's TV programme. Breathless with excitement, Annabel was already recording what they had 'seen'. Peter slipped out after Chooker.

Wandering down the corridors, Chooker felt lost and miserable. What was wrong with her? She sagged against a wall. Why wasn't she chirpy and bright as usual, excited to see new things and people? Eh, she knew the answer, of course. With Prentast in danger, she couldn't be easy. In this House, where was the private place? She had to think.

A hand touched her arm, startling her. Peter was looking rather worried. 'Okay, Chooker?' he asked. 'Yoo okay?'

She shrugged. Not really.

A huge bird-boat flew roaring over the House. Peter beckoned Chooker to a window to watch it settle with a long splash on the sea in front of the House. A boat shot out from the shore and several new Giants were brought ashore from the flying boat, some carrying large camcorders, all talking eagerly, their breath puffing white as they tramped and skidded up the icy slope. Doctormurry came out of his room to greet them at the door, shaking their hands in welcome. He beckoned Chooker and Peter, but Chooker backed away down the passage. Their voices faded as a door closed.

'Teevee men!' Peter said, grinning encouragement. 'Foryoo! Doctormurry mustev cawldem laznite. Ant Annabel elgoh ballistic.'

Blankly Chooker shrugged. Peter wanted to help, she was sure, but she didn't know what he was trying to tell her, and she couldn't think with him there.

She suddenly realized that she didn't need to think. There was only one thing to do. She had to go home. Yes, it was silly, spending so much strain and pain on getting here and then running straight away again—but she must go, and at once, before Prentast could be driven to sacrifice herself. She had been right to come—of course she had! But things had changed. Now she had to go back. Eh, she'd get such a scolding—but she'd known that before she came. She must go, as soon as she could. She could come again, as soon as she had put things right.

Would Mungith leave with her? He seemed happier here than she was. And what would he tell the Council? He still trusted Hemminal, he might not back her up.

Once in the caves, she'd find her way home. But where

was the cave entrance? And she needed her warm clothes again. Maybe Peter would really help. If he told, and she was stopped . . .

Well, she just had to convince him.

She smiled at him, and took his hand, trying to send thoughts as well as words. 'Peter, ie goh too Atlantis. Tawk too Prentastal yoo heer. Annabel sister Bil? Okay. Prentastal sister mee. Ie noh goh, Hemminal get Prentastal ded. Ie goh —' How did you say 'right away' in Giant words? She wished she had paid more attention to learning words, like Mungith. Frustrated, she acted running.

'Hemminal—hooz Hemminal?' Peter held up a hand. 'Hangon, Chooker. Stop.' He took a deep breath, trying to remember what words she knew. 'Yoo wantoo goh too Atlantis?' She nodded. 'Okay! Ile goh too Atlantis with yoo! Yoo, mee—' he waved a hand to draw them together—'wee goh too Atlantis! Okay? Okay! Ile get sootz, bootz—'

Chooker could scarcely believe it. Was it that easy? Did he really mean it? That he would help her? Go with her? Her little face lit up with glee, and she gripped his hands. 'Okay! Okay!'

Doctormurry came out into the corridor and called, 'Chooker! Chooker!' He seemed excited and happy, but he felt somehow like a Moray eel, grinning out of its hole at a crab it was just going to pounce on. Eh, Bastiyyal take him! She'd have to go and see what he wanted.

She put a finger to her lips. 'Noh tawk wee goh!'

Peter winked at her. 'Yookidding? Noh, noh! Sh! Okay!'

Enthralled by the antics of the Giant children and monsters on the teevee, Mungith didn't notice Chooker and Peter return with Doctormurry until a snap in Annabel's voice made him jump and look round. 'Wot, press?' She was furious, shaking her head, scolding Doctormurry.

'Toldyoo!' Peter whispered to Chooker, grinning.

Annabel's lips were tight as the King Giant beckoned Mungith to come along with him and Chooker. 'Wee goh owt? Okay. Eh, teevee good! Thankyoo, Annabel!' With watching the flickering box, Mungith's head and eyes were aching and blurred; he begged another pain-stop pill from Chooker, and came along readily. The King Giant had been suspicious of strangers, but no more than he should be, less than Shark Father had been of Bil. It was actually reassuring that they hadn't been welcomed too heartily by everyone, which might have meant a trap.

The Hall was full of Giants, including some new ones, Mungith thought, though it was hard to tell them apart. They were all grinning in delight, and some were pointing huge camcorders at the youngsters. Confidently, Mungith grinned back.

'Mungithak and Chooker!' Doctormurry announced, his hands on their shoulders.

The Giants clapped. Mungith blinked, startled by the sign of respect; but then the Giants started shouting and flashing lights.

Blinded, terrified, Chooker twisted out of Doctormurry's grip, snatched her knife from her neck so fast she snapped the thong, slashed at his hand as he snatched at her arm, and fled out of the door and down the corridor. Feet pattered behind her—she spun round, knife ready, to find Peter racing after her. 'Okay, Chooker!' he gasped. 'Okay!'

He was alone. No one else was chasing her. Puffing, she realized she had been silly. Giants always shouted a lot, and needed a lot of light.

Peter was nodding, beckoning. 'K'mawn! Thail tawk too Mungithak, eet, drink. Doctormurry, teevee men. Letz goh now, wile thair bizzy!' He drew her into the bedroom he shared with his aunt.

For a moment she hesitated. Go? Go now? Yes, yes! While everyone was occupied. They'd think she had gone to hide, and they wouldn't worry about her. If they were talking to Mungith, that would keep him off her trail for a while too. Yes!

Peter was pulling open doors and drawers, dumping things on a bed—boots, warm socks and mitts, leggings and tunics, his red tube suit and Annabel's yellow one, a big tawch. 'K'mawn!'

Suddenly full of energy again, Chooker copied him as he dressed. His leggings and tunic and suit were too big for her, as Annabel's were on him, and the spare fabric and queer shapes clung to odd places and rolled comically at their wrists and ankles, but it was all incredibly warm.

She grinned at Peter. 'K'mawn!'

12

Mungith backed rapidly towards the door, whipped out his knife, and stood poised to defend Chooker's retreat. The Giants were pointing their camcorders' snouts at him. The brilliant lights flashed again and again, dazzling—but he wasn't hurt.

Annabel was ready to hurry out after Chooker. Doctormurry, sucking a bleeding hand, was calling to her, scolding her and telling her to stay. He smiled tightly. 'Okay, Mungithak! Okay!'

Warily, Mungith relaxed. Nobody was threatening him. The flashes were coming from the camcorders. Maybe they needed extra light to copy people? How silly Chook would feel, being scared of just lights! Peter would calm her down and bring her back to apologize.

'Mungithak,' Doctormurry said, obviously introducing him to the new Giants. He smiled rather condescendingly, between sucks at the cut on his hand, and named some of them. 'Jimmipaterson, Kevinbremner, Alisonmacray, Benrangaheeree.'

At last, people with a decent length of name! Mungithak bowed politely to each of them, fingers to chest. 'Benrangaheeree, Kevinbremner, Alisonmacray, Jimmipaterson.' Their jaws dropped; they'd never have managed to remember all those names. Pleased to have impressed them, he bowed again. 'Hunter Mungithak, Male Adult of Point House.'

Benrangaheeree tried to repeat the name, but 'Akvillawsenniyyak Mungithak triyssowni jeellayzior Breezingusmine' was beyond him. 'Mungithak,' Mungith said kindly.

The new Giants looked relieved. 'Hi, Mungithak!' they chorused, and started calling, 'Shaikhands!'

Doctormurry held out his hand. Mungith looked at it blankly. Was he supposed to give him a present, or lick the cut too? Doctormurry grasped his hand and waved it up and down, while the lights flashed again. Hand-holding must be a greeting, like bowing. Beaming, Doctormurry turned to face the lights, his hand on Mungith's shoulder.

All the new Giants started asking questions. When she could get a word in past Doctormurry's chatter, Annabel answered them. Once she snapped, 'No! Itwoz Bil!' and went on vehemently to explain, almost shouting down Doctormurry who was arguing with her. What bad Manners! Mungith grinned; if they were children, Mother would spank the lot of them! And if they were proper Adults, a dozen duels would have been called for already.

The Cook brought in the Giants' favourite hot drinks, tee and cawfy, which Mungith found equally nasty. 'Tryacokesun,' the Cook said, offering him a metal jar with a hole in the top. Mungith sniffed it doubtfully, tasted the sweet-sharp fizzy water inside, and wrinkled his nose when it prickled. Everybody laughed. Should he take offence? No, you couldn't expect Giants to know any better. He grinned round. 'Okay, tryacokesun good!' They laughed again.

Annabel patted Mungith's shoulder. 'Okay? Ie goh fined Chooker.' She went out.

Mungith was eager to talk, when the Giants asked something he could understand. They seemed quite like real people, interested and noisy, their camcorders working non-stop. Chooker would have been useful, to sense for him; but he managed, with hands and the words he had learned. His eyes sparkled with enjoyment; he was the centre of attention!

109

He was keen to boast about his home, to display his tattoo and knife. The Giants darkened the room, exclaimed at his skin and glow-tube and tried to copy the shine with their camcorders.

Benrangaheeree was talking to Doctormurry. 'Wot?' He swung round to Mungith. 'Yoo can tawk mentally?' He pointed to his head and Mungith's. 'In hed?'

Mungith grinned. 'Noh, noh. Chooker tawk in hed. Not mee.' They were excited, but he hadn't enough words to explain that being able to link minds was rare.

'Big nife,' Kevinbremner commented. 'Yoo fite with nife?' He gestured to show what he meant.

'Yes, yes!' In spite of the awkward neck support Mungith drew his knife and went through the first of the six warm-up exercises. Impressed, Kevinbremner and the other new Giants flashed lots of lights at it.

Annabel came back, looking rather worried, but Doctormurry irritably hushed her. The Giants wanted to ask her about Chooker's ability to talk mentally, and she was soon fully occupied with them. Then for a long time the new Giants made Mungith stand beside King Doctormurry while they flashed lights and pointed the camcorders at them, and Doctormurry talked. And talked. And talked.

Mungith started to get bored. His eyes were blurring and his head hurt. He sat down at a table and took another pain-stop with the last of his tryacokesun. Only three left. Eh well, he wouldn't need many more, he was getting better. But he'd rest for a minute . . .

At first, everything went well. Peter got Chooker out of the Giant City as smoothly as if he'd planned it for tides. He gleefully nipped into a store room to grab some food to stow in Chooker's pack—'Immerjensy rashunz!'—and opened a door to Outside.

Chooker froze. The openness, the space! She would fall up, up into the roof!

'K'mawn, Chooker!' Peter encouraged her. 'Taik mie hand. K'mawn!'

No! No . . . Yes! If a Giant could do it, so could she! And if she wanted to go home, she had to. Chooker gripped Peter's arm till he winced, and forced herself out. He helped her scramble blindly over the icy rocks behind the Giant houses, bent double to hide her face from Rassiyyak. At the end of the group of buildings she collapsed shivering. She couldn't go out, not right out there!

Grinning, Peter freed his arm. 'Yoo stay heer! I get skidoo. Okay?' She couldn't move, anyway. She clung to a rock to hold herself down. This was stupid. But she couldn't stop the panic cutting off her breath, thundering in her chest, knotting her stomach . . .

Not far off, a couple of small land-boats were tied to a rail. Peter walked openly down to untie one and rode it back. 'K'mawn, Chooker! K'mawn!' Somehow she drove herself forward to climb up behind him. 'Okay!' he chortled in triumph, and urged the boat, the skidoo, forward, over the hill and out of sight of the houses.

Nobody had noticed. They were away!

Chooker knew she'd never have managed it by herself. She was almost blind, even though a mist high under the roof cut down Rassiyak's dreadful glare quite a lot. Her arms tight as octopus tentacles round Peter's waist, she jounced along, hoping that he knew where he was going, because she didn't, not in this dazzling expanse of shimmering, shivering white.

Gradually, very gradually, she relaxed. As long as she didn't look up, she began to almost enjoy the ride. Almost. It was icy cold on her face, and her breath froze her nose.

At last Peter stopped the boat and tugged her up a flight of steps cut in ice, round a corner of a cliff to point to a crack in the rocks. While she dived in he hesitated, looking back; then told himself aloud, 'Go for it!' and followed her.

Inside, the darkness fell like feathers on Chooker's aching eyes. With a huge sigh of relief she pulled off the lenses, rubbed away the itch, and grinned at Peter. She was going home, and much quicker and easier than her trip out had been! 'Okay, good, okay! K'mawn!'

Peter knew the path through the first few caves, and when he faltered Chooker had started remembering the turns and passages to the slide where they had first met. Yes, there were the faint traces of footprints. It wasn't as complicated a route as up through the Lichen Caves. As she skidded down the rolling scree, she laughed out loud. 'K'mawn!' She tugged her heavy clogs off, to leave just her comfortable sandals, cupped her hands beside her eyes to cut down the light of Peter's tawch behind her, and skipped off.

At first, Peter trotted enthusiastically after her. He'd be famous! 'Teenager Contacts New Civilization! Atlantis Found by Young Hero! Discovery of the Century!' he shouted out loud, laughing when Chooker turned to stare in surprise. It was a terrific thrill, like an adventure film.

He'd been raging when his mother shut the car boot on his hand and broke several of the bones, just when his teacher had said he had a real chance of the Junior Championship at the South Island Tae Kwon Do Tournament—he'd been practising really hard. Mum had organized the visit to Scott Base to make up for missing the tournament. The man next door worked on an Antarctic tour ship; he'd been going to take his wife on a trip, at staff rates, but she got mumps, and Mum had asked if Peter could take her place, stay over in Scott Base, and come back with the next ship—and somehow she'd managed to swing it. It had probably cost a bomb.

He'd thought it might be not too bad, with skiing and snowballs. But it had been boring. Everybody was working all day at their scientific experiments, chasing him away from the sensitive equipment. Even the five or six short caving trips in Aunt Annabel's spare time, to try to trace his uncle, hadn't been as exciting as he had hoped—well, not till the last one! This was far better. Mum had done him a good turn after all. His mates at school would be green with envy! He imagined the TV interviews he'd give. This was great!

Round the beam of the torch the black weight of rock pressed in and down on him. He'd not be beaten, though. He was tough—the toughest boy in his class, even if he was about the smallest. Losers don't try, winners don't quit, Dad said. He'd not quit, no way! He shouted into all the side caves to ring the echoes, sang and whistled.

But it went on too long. Despite himself, the songs faded away. The air grew thick, hard to breathe, let alone sing. He began to lag behind. Where Chooker slipped easily through narrow gaps, skipped over and slid under rocks, he squeezed and hesitated. These heavy boots gave him blisters. Jogging or potholing would be more use here than tae kwon do. They had been scrambling through this blind black maze for hours. How much longer? How much further?

Simultaneously Chooker realized that she had reached the crack back into the old mines, and that the light of the tawch had gone entirely.

Rather irritated, she went back. Peter was walking slowly, limping, the tawch drooping in his hand. Giffaral was right—men were useless in mines! She opened her mouth to snap at him, tell him to hurry up—and then shut it. She wasn't being fair.

Peter was really doing very well. He wasn't used to being in caves at all. Outside, she had felt terrified she would fly away up into the roof if she looked up or lifted her feet off the ground. This was the same thing in reverse. Besides, she was going home; he was heading away from his own world. He had been kind to her, helped her. She must do the same for him.

She sat down and beckoned him to sit by her. He dropped, twitching. She hugged him without speaking and reached out her mind to him. He wanted the contact, and the link came easily. *Calm, still . . . no worries . . . relax . . . no fear . . . safe here . . . okay, okay . . .*

We're lost! Peter couldn't help it. *Can't breathe—we'll never be found . . .*

No, no! This is my home. We're all right. Okay, okay . . .

I'm a coward.

No, you're not! She rejected the idea with scorn. *You're scared, but that's natural. A coward wouldn't have come. You're brave!*

At last the trembling stopped. He drew a deep breath, sniffed hard, and rubbed a wrist across his mouth, and managed a half-grin. *Losers don't try, winners don't quit. Okay?*

'Okay!'

He shook his head, though. 'Foot sore.' He felt as if his blisters had blisters.

Eh, Bastiyyal! Giants were so soft! 'Giv mee foot.' Pulling off his heavy boots, she hissed in alarm. Blisters on his heels and toes, several broken—what a mess! But his courage in coming so far without complaint impressed her. 'Peter wawk on sore foot too here, okay, good, okay!' She rubbed them with her first-aid stick, and cut strips from a tunic as bandages.

She opened her pack. 'Wee eet.' Mother said people always felt better after food.

It was true. After they had eaten and rested, Peter pushed himself to his feet without being urged. Chooker could feel his fear, but he grinned cockily. 'K'mawn, then! Okay?'

He really was brave. 'Peter okay. Peter good.' She clapped to encourage him.

When she led him crawling under the crack and into the old mine workings, she pointed down the tunnel. 'Atlantis thair. Mungith, mee, wee kum thair. Wee goh. Okay?'

Peter puffed in relief. It couldn't be too far now. Could it?

In the bigger tunnel the light was too bright. 'Stop tawch, eh?'

Peter grimaced, but switched off the torch. He stiffened in the heavy darkness. Chooker gripped his hand. *Okay, don't worry! You can see. It's not all black. Look, see the glow?* 'Yoo see? Yes?' Slowly, as his eyes adapted to the lack of light, he realized that yes, he could see. A dim orange tunnel stretched away round a corner. Beside him Chooker was smiling with white teeth in a golden face. 'Yoo see? Okay?'

'Okay!' This was like playing 'Doom' at the darkest setting, following dim tunnels you couldn't see the end of, but it was better than working with just a torch in a black hole. He pointed along the tunnel. 'Thair? That way?'

'Thair,' she confirmed, and led him limping off again. They still had a long way to go.

13

A clatter of chairs startled Mungith awake. The cook was serving a meal. What bad Manners, to fall asleep while the King was talking! But everyone was smiling. Giants weren't fussy about Manners. Eh, he felt ever so much better after that snooze! He didn't see double any longer—great!

The new Giants wanted Mungith to use the spiky fork thing. It kept your fingers clean, but it dribbled sauce; after a while he went back to the proper spoon and fingers.

The Giants grinned in a superior way.

They were sneering at him! All Mungithak's pleasure in the attention shown him withered. He felt mortified; how dared they condescend to him, the great hulking bad-Mannered brutes! Eh, Beliyyak drown them all! He was sorry he'd ever come. He wished he had Chooker there. He'd strangle her—but even his little cousin would be a comfort.

Where was Chooker, anyway? Now that he thought about it, he was surprised that she hadn't got over her fright and come back to talk to the Giants—she was the one who had wanted to in the first place, after all. And Peter would surely have brought her back for the meal. He looked over to Annabel. 'Wairz Chooker?'

She shrugged, frowning. 'With Peter. Thay goh owt.'

Outside? Under the eye of Rassiyyak? Mungith whistled; well done, Chooker! Eh, well. If she was with Peter, she'd be all right.

The door opened and two more Giants came in. One grinned over at Annabel. 'Dintseeyoo kumbak,' he said cheerfully.

'Kumbak?' Annabel was puzzled.

He nodded, saying something Mungith didn't grasp.

Annabel jumped to her feet. 'Skidoo? Notmee!' she yelped. 'Mustevbeen Peter! Peter and Chooker! Wen?'

What had Chooker and Peter done? Mungith's heart suddenly jumped painfully. She couldn't have tried to go home, could she? To save Prentast? With just Peter? Without him? Could she?

Beliyyak take the little sea-squirt, yes, she could!

The Giants were all exclaiming, arguing. 'Serch awlohver!' the King ordered, and some hurried out. What would they do? What should he do?

He had to go after the silly cavy! She'd get into trouble without him. She always did. He had to stop her. Look after her. Eh, he'd murder her! Well, no . . .

He'd need help. He touched Annabel's arm. She glanced down; 'Yes, yes, Mungithak, okay! Weel fined them!'

He hung on until, tutting irritably, she gave him some attention. 'Chooker goh too Atlantis. Chooker and Peter goh.'

'Atlantis!' Annabel didn't seem to have considered this, but finally she nodded.

'Ie now goh too Atlantis, fined Chooker and Peter,' he told her. 'Yoo giv me hawt—' What was Giantish for clothes? In frustration, he jerked her tunic sleeve. 'Yoo and mee, wee goh wair yoo fined me and Chooker. Ie goh Atlantis. Ie fined Peter. Peter kum here.'

Doctormurry shook his head. 'Koodbee ennywair!'

But Annabel nodded abruptly. 'Okay. Yoo goh too Atlantis, fined Peter. Mee too. Ile goh too Atlantis with yoo.'

Uproar exploded. For some reason the Giants seemed shocked at this idea.

Mungith had his own problems. Did he want to take another Giant down into the City? When the first one had done so much damage? Eh well, Peter was already on his way. And he didn't see how he could stop her. Not if he wanted her help.

The Giants' noisy argument showed no signs of stopping. Annabel wanted to go with him, protesting, 'Ie goh pawtholing!' The new Giants seemed to want to stop her and come instead. Doctormurry was forbidding anybody to go anywhere.

Mungithak shrugged, tugged Annabel's arm again, and headed for the door. 'Wee goh now!'

'Organized serchfirst!' Doctormurry declared.

'Okay, okay!' Annabel glared. 'Yoo organize yoor serch heer. Ile chek the caiv, see if the skidooz thair. Saivtime later.' She marched out, leaving him squawking. Mungith trotted after her, glad to be moving. But she mustn't come!

In Mungith's bedroom, she faced him grimly. 'Yoo okay? Not tired?'

He ripped off the stiff collar. 'Ie okay.' He frowned up at her. 'Yoo big, big. Caiv down, down.' He showed her the height of the tunnels, not quite hip-height on her. 'In caiv, yoo—' he went down on hands and knees, to show how she'd have to crawl. 'Sore leg, sore hed, sore back, sore foot. Yoo stop, ie noh stop.' Maybe that would scare her off.

She simply flung open a cupboard door and started hauling out clothes. 'Wee goh now, okay? Okay. K'mawn!'

Chooker was worried. The air was astonishingly warm and steamy, so that she and Peter had to pause to take off layers of clothes before they melted. She could move more easily without the clinging tubes wrapped round her arms and legs, but the damp heat must be from the burst. How big was it?

Though Peter's glasses kept steaming up, and he complained, 'Yuk!' at the growing stink of sulphur, he was feeling better. The roof was just above his head; he had to look out for low bits, but on the whole he could walk upright, and it obviously wasn't closing in on him. When he told himself that above the ankles he felt fine, he could almost believe it.

Eventually they passed a tide-mark where the burst had risen and then receded. The light faded, for the lower algae had been covered by a layer of mud, but Chooker was pleased. If the water had sunk they might be able to splash straight through. Sweat was trickling down her spine. What was that heavy plopping noise? 'Tawch,' she suggested, wiping her face, and winced as Peter started the gush of light.

In front of them lay a pool of thick greyish-yellow liquid. As they watched, it suddenly spouted, blowing a gout of mud up to splatter the roof. And again, in a different place. And again. The tunnel roof dipped right under the surface of the simmering flood. There was no way past. And they were still quite a long way from the entrance to the mine where she had come in. How far had it flooded? Not right down to the City, surely? No, they'd have stopped it long before that.

Dismayed, Peter turned accusing eyes on Chooker. 'Wotnow, eh?'

'Wee goh—' Slightly puzzled, she showed 'round' with her hands. There was always another cave.

Peter's shoulders sagged, but he gritted his teeth. Winners don't quit!

Chooker sniffed. Huh! But of course, it must be easier Outside, where even if some of the roof fell there would still be plenty of space to climb over the rocks. 'K'mawn!'

The stolen skidoo was parked outside the cave. Annabel huffed with relief, fright, and anger. Chooker and Peter were in here. Wait till she caught that boy!

Mungith dived into the darkness like a dodo chick diving under its mother's wings. Inside, he pulled off the goggles. Eh, it was so good to be in decent light again! He peered round; six openings. He looked to Annabel for direction. 'This way,' she beckoned, and he hurried after her.

It was over a dozen sixty-paces to the scree slope. Mungith peered down the hole; yes, this was where he had been knocked out. From here on, he could find the way. He turned to Annabel, and bowed deeply. 'Ie goh now. Ie kumbak timorra, timorra.' He hoped she'd take the hint and stay . . .

She was staring past him in fright. He whipped up and round, staggering as his head suddenly pounded, and clutched at Annabel for support. She lurched forward on to the scree and skidded down it, screaming, while he tumbled after her in a roaring cascade of stones and gravel.

At the bottom she sat up, cursing painfully, groping frantically for the light. For a wonder, it wasn't broken. She lit up the furthest corner, the hole where Chooker and Mungith had come in, gripped Mungith's arm and pointed. 'Nife! Get owt yoor nife!' she hissed.

After a long minute, behind the rocks, a bright black eye appeared.

Mungith studied the eye. It blinked, and became two eyes, beady, intelligent, scared . . . 'High-Whisker! You didn't run away! Okay, Annabel, okay! High-Whisker, come on, fine rat, well done!' He snapped his fingers to call the big rat, grinning and going gently to meet him. 'High-Whisker! That's right—it's me, Mungith, remember me?'

Annabel sat rigid as the rat inched forward to sniff Mungith's fingers and lick them. It began jumping about in delight. Okay? She didn't think rats the size of Alsatians were okay. However, it seemed more scared of her than she was of it, shying away from the light.

'How did you miss Chooker?' As High-Whisker rubbed against his legs, sniffing up at his face, the fishy smell of the rat's breath gave Mungith a clue. 'Away finding food, eh? A pool with shrimps or crabs? Eh, it's good to see you!'

120

The monstrous beast obviously knew Mungith. Puffing in relief, Annabel tried to stand up—and sank back with a yelp. Her left ankle was not just bruised, like the rest of her; it was sprained. Badly.

However desperately she wanted to, she couldn't continue.

Oh, what would Peter's mother say if he was lost?

Mungith stared at her in dismay as she fought to control her fear and anger. At last she forced herself to smile tightly at him. 'Yoo gowon, Mungith, fined Peter.' It was the only thing to do. 'Ile sit here. Ie noh goh back, thail kum, fined mee. Yoo goh get Peter. Kumback with Peter timorra, okay? Pleez! Gowon!'

Mungith was glad she had so much sense. She was safe enough, huge and strong, warmly dressed, with the tawch to scare off wild rats till the other Giants came. And Chooker might need him. Might? Would! 'Farewell, Annabel Winston. May the Little Gods watch over you—but not too closely!' He bowed to her in respect, swung on to High-Whisker's back—the saddle was gone; well, you couldn't expect two miracles in one tide—took a good grip of the rat's neck fur and urged him into a dead run down the tunnel.

Behind him, Annabel bit her knuckles to stop herself screaming for him to come back. It had taken all her strength to send him on, to stay alone in this hole, in pain. Rescuers might take a long time to find her through the maze of tunnels . . .

She'd not sit waiting to be collected like a parcel. After a while, wincing, she started to push herself back up the slope. She thought it would take her mind off worrying about Peter. She was wrong.

Chooker and Peter tried all the side tunnels in turn, back along the old mine. The first stopped after an hour's trek, at a worked-out coal face. The second looked as if it should go on, but a huge boulder had slipped from the roof to block it. Peter limped on gamely. 'Next, okay?'

As they laboured along the third tunnel, Chooker stopped, held up a hand for silence.

From away ahead, a faint tapping was echoing. People! Probably building a barrier wall against the flood—

Peter's head came round. 'Lissen!' He pointed to his ear, and then behind them.

Chooker strained to hear. The tapping ahead. Their breathing. Behind them, a hint of Mungith—wishful thinking, that must be. And something else.

A scraping, scratching noise. Claws on rock. Heavy claws. Wild rats—killers.

Chooker's heart froze. She drew her knife. 'Goh! Goh now! Gowon!' No time for limping! 'Goh!' She hustled Peter forward, fumbling in her pouch as the scutter of claws came nearer. Everybody who heard a child's help-call would come running to the rescue. Even if the people along the tunnel didn't hear the shrill whistle, it couldn't hurt, and it might scare off the rats.

Peter yelled something and switched on the tawch, pointing it backwards. Down the passage there was a squeal of fright, a scuffle of claws.

'Good, Peter! Okay!' Chooker shouted. Maybe the light would keep the rats off till they reached the people ahead. 'K'mawn!' Screwing up her eyes, blowing her whistle whenever she had breath, she urged him to run on as fast as he could see.

Forgetting his blisters, Peter did his best, but the tawch didn't help. It dazzled them both now, and he had to keep pointing it backwards so that his eyes were blinded by the contrast between its light and the blackness of the tunnel. He couldn't see at all where he was going, and stumbled and tripped as he ran.

Ahead there was light, voices shouting in alarm. Behind

them the claws started again—but help was near. 'Gowon, Peter!' Chooker screamed.

People were running towards them. Coals, a couple of Blocks, a Granite, their skins glowing gently, their eyes wincing from the tawch light, their hands full of picks and spades and knives. 'Help! Rats!' Chooker yelled.

Behind her a disgusted voice shouted, 'Don't be daft! It's me!'

14

Chooker skidded to a stop and gaped. 'Mungith! How . . . how did you—?' She could scarcely speak.

'Following you to keep you out of trouble as usual! Idiot!'

'But how did you follow me—and find the turn-off—'

'High-Whisker. He waited for you, and I rode him here. He scented where you'd turned off.'

'High-Whisker?' Yes, there he was, panting gently, flinching from the light. *Wonderful High-Whisker! Champion rat of the caves!* High-Whisker sniffed in delight at her hands, proudly whiffled his nose, sat down and started to groom himself. He was back with people, and they were pleased. They'd look after him now.

'Peter, yoo okay?' Chooker smiled to the young Giant.

'Okay, okay!' Panting, grinning, Peter was staring at High-Whisker in awe. 'Rat—' his gesture showed he meant High-Whisker—'Rat okay!'

Chooker looked up for her rescuers. Behind Mungith and Peter half a dozen Blocks, the masons of Atlantis, a couple of big Granites, and several Coals were standing in a tight group, their eyes huge.

Fear.

Their emotion shocked Chooker rigid. She hadn't thought! She had got so used to Giants' height, even in these few tides, and Peter was a small Giant. 'Eh, thank you for coming to my whistle! You know me—Chooker, Point First Daughter? And Mungithak? We found the Giants! This is a boy Giant.'

Horror.

'There's no danger!' Mungith reassured them. 'I was like you, I thought Giants were all bad people, but they aren't.'

Terror.

Chooker couldn't think to them, she was too tired. She walked towards them, urgently pleading, trying to cut through the glaze of dread that blanked their faces and eyes. 'We must speak to the Queen. Hemminal murdered Giffaral, and she broke the mine too, I saw her—' She was almost touching them.

Panic.

A shovel swung. Peter yelled a warning. Too late.

Stunned, Chooker slid to the floor of the tunnel.

Mungith had leapt forward, trying to stop the blow. A Granite swung a spade at his head, and the edge sliced down into the fist he threw up to save himself. He spun away, nursing his hand, and four Blocks dived on to his back. Peter tried to go forward to help, until the picks and a couple of long knives rose to threaten him. He could only stand and watch as Mungith was overpowered.

Peter wasn't afraid. These frighteningly strong little people had grabbed him with tough, horny hands, lifted Chooker's unconscious body as easily as if she were a baby, had driven him and Mungithak stooping and crawling along low, cramped tunnels and forced them into a skin canoe towed behind a bigger boat. Afraid? No. He was terrified. He sat frozen, trying to keep breathing against a horrible tightness in his chest.

At least the Giant wasn't going to panic and upset the boat, Mungith judged. He sighed. He should have realized what would happen. People wouldn't listen to Chooker— well, he hadn't himself. Probably only what she'd said about Hemminal had saved their lives. What would happen when they reached the City?

For the first time it sank in; he had threatened Chooker with being thrown out of Death Gate, but it was actually possible for him, too.

In the bottom of the canoe Chooker twitched, moaned. Her eyes blinked blindly and found a rather blurred face bending anxiously above her. 'Mung . . . '

'I'm here. You'll be all right, Chook. I'll look after you.' As far as he could.

'Mung.' Trembling, she blinked up. 'Mungith—eh, Mungith . . . Eh, look, you're bleeding all over me. Your hand—'

'What?' Mungith held up his right hand, blood oozing through the scrap of his tunic that he had wrapped round it. 'I've lost the outside two fingers. I didn't feel it in the fight.' It hurt now, though. So did his head, and bruises all over. He had taken the last pain-stop, but it had worn off during the two hour journey. 'I've used up your gelstick. Sorry.'

She gave him a wavering smile. As if that mattered! She leaned against him, slowly recovering.

As time passed and he wasn't killed, Peter felt better too. His weariness and aches faded. Even his feet hurt less. He began to stare round, exclaiming, 'Lookit that!' at the colours of the passing caverns, the towing dolphins, the locks in the long, twisting waterway, everything.

Mungith wished the boy would be quiet. He was disturbing Chook.

As the boats finally turned into the City channel, the vault of the main cavern ahead boomed and echoed with the noise of many, many people. At the quayside two long boats were moored, draped in red to carry the Queen to her sacrifice. 'Death barges! For Prentast?' Chooker stiffened. 'We can't be too late!'

'No, they haven't left yet, the flags are still up!' Mungith reassured her. 'We're in time.' Though what they could do, he didn't know.

The barge cast off the towline and swept off to the Coal quay, leaving the canoe bobbing in the middle of the central harbour basin. Word of the Giant spread rapidly. Without paddles, Chooker, Mungith, and Peter could only sit and suffer the blast of hostility from the crowds filling the harbour flat and the terraces, stamping and screaming curses down at the little boat that dipped and tilted gently on the silver-blue water. The echoing roar startled the petrels and cormorants from every ledge of the immense cavern to add their screeches to the din.

Peter gritted his teeth and concentrated on hiding his fear. Chooker clutched Mungith's rigid arm and cowered as the crowd's rage assaulted her mind.

On the quayside Hemminal, the tall dark woman who had begun to haunt Chooker's dreams, pushed through to the front of the crowd. Behind her in the path she opened followed a man in a long white tunic. King Pyroonak gestured for silence, shouting against the deafening noise. Finally he waved forward Shevirrak, the old Priest of the Little Gods, and the long, mournful booming of the ancient shell horn slowly, slowly subdued the uproar till at last Pyroonak could make himself heard.

'Wilder!' he roared.

A roar of applause started the birds screaming again. 'Wilder! Wilder! Wilder!' the crowd started to chant, till the King held up an arm to silence them again.

'Chooker, Mungithak, of Point House, you have defied the Council, and brought another Giant into the City! I name you both Wilder! Wilder and Outcast! You will be cast out of Death Gate, you and this abomination!'

The bellow of applause was even stronger. At length Pyroonak raised his hand to still it. 'Hunters, come forward!' The Hunters, who were called on to deal with any disturbance in the City, began to push through to the front of the crowd.

This might be Chooker's only chance. Before the shouting could rise again, she pushed herself to her feet, balancing precariously, and screamed, 'Murder! Murder! Murder!' In the sudden hush, she yelled, 'I accuse Hemminal of Kelp House! She murdered Giffaral of Coal House!'

'Liar!' Hemminal shouted. 'Traitor! Outcast!'

'Bastiyyal witness my words!' Chooker screeched at the top of her voice. 'She broke the mine, opened the gusher! I saw her!' She steadied herself as the canoe wobbled.

'Outcast!' Hemminal's eyes found the rest of her House and her crew, and they began to yell too. 'Outcast! Outcast!' The clamour spread.

But everyone had heard the accusation. 'Stop! We want to hear this!' the Coals shouted, ignoring the King's glare.

From the quayside a Block bellowed, 'I've just come from the mines! The burst's not as big as they said, and going down!' Some Coals and a couple of his House supported him.

'Out with the Outcasts!' Pyroonak shouted. 'Hunters, take them away!'

Hemminal's crew stepped forward, but many Hunters hung back uneasily, arguing. 'His sister, of course he'd back her—No, he wouldn't!—Can't trust a Kelp!—You calling my cousin a liar?' Squabbles broke out all through the crowd.

Hemminal slid down into her boat, moored just below her by the quay. Her rage at the opposition, the accusation, filled her mind with red fury. If she could kill the brat now, before she blabbed—Pyroonak would get her off—who'd care, the child was Outcast anyway . . . Nobody attacked her and got away with it. She lifted a harpoon.

Mungith's eyes were blurring again, but he peered over, watching Hemminal like a gannet watching a fish; he knew her. He saw the cast, and flung himself wildly at Chooker. The canoe capsized. The harpoon flew exactly where Chooker's chest had been, as all three youngsters splashed yelling into the water.

A harbour shark cruised over, black fin slicing the silver ripples . . . but two dolphins were already zipping to the rescue. Saving silly people who fell off boats was fun. To Peter's astonishment, a grinning head popped up between him and Chooker as they spluttered to the surface, and a hard dorsal fin nudged his hand, offering a tow. Swimming with dolphins! He'd never expected this! His spirits suddenly lifted. Somehow a good deal happier he helped Chooker to squelch up the quay steps, grinned at Mungith heaving himself wearily from the water behind him, and stared in awe at the varied shapes and sizes of the small people crowding all round.

Shocked protests—'What was that? Who threw it? She had no right! Not fair!'—intensified the din, until the old Priest sounded his horn again. Slowly, the noise faded. At the rear of the crowd, a respectful clapping drew eyes from the three dripping youngsters.

All in sacrificial red, her tall head-dress towering above the rest, Queen Prentastal led a small procession of all the Mothers and Fathers following the King down from the Council Hall. Distom, Point Father, was carried in a chair with a Silver attendant. Point Mother, very stately and dramatic in coppery lace, clinking gently in all her jewellery, abandoned formality to run forward to hug Chooker, her eyes brimming with tears.

Chooker almost sobbed in relief. Distom and Mother would make it all right!

Stern-faced, Prentastal stopped beside Pyroonak. 'King Pyroonak, you have declared Chooker, Point First Daughter, to be a Wilder.' Prentastal's tone and words were cold and formal, and she carefully didn't look at Chooker; she must not show any bias. 'You have no right to do this.'

Gritting his teeth, Pyroonak shook his head. 'I decided, as King—'

'But the Council makes that decision, not the King alone.'

The Mothers and Fathers behind her murmured agreement. 'Also, no children can be declared Wilder. Their own Father and Mother must first declare them Adult, disown them as uncontrollable. Point Mother, Point Father, do you so disown your First Daughter?'

Mother's arms were round both Chooker and Mungith. She shook her head till her ear-chain and hair ornaments jingled. 'No, Queen Prentastal, we do not.' Her rich contralto rang out clearly across the hushed cavern. 'Chooker is self-willed and obstinate, but breaks no Custom for fun, gain, or malice. Whatever she has done, she believed she had good reason for. I thought I had lost all my daughters . . . ' Her voice trembled on a near-sob. She drew a deep breath, and smiled to her youngest child. 'Chooker is still a loved and respected daughter of Point House, as Mungithak is a valued and honourable Adult.' Saving his strength, Distom nodded agreement.

Chooker's face started to crumple. Such support, when if she was found guilty all her House would be despised for upholding her! She bit her lip, sniffed hard, and found Mungith taking her hand. 'Chin up, Point First Daughter!' he whispered. 'Don't let Point House down!'

Distom was smiling gently to them. He wouldn't speak to Chooker mentally, in case another Senser picked it up and he was accused of coaching her, but he was sending them his love. Mungith nodded to Peter. 'Okay, Peter! See Prentastal, Distom, Feelissal? Thay good. Wee okay!' Peter certainly hoped he was right.

'Very well,' Prentastal said. 'A Kelp Adult is accused of murder, and a counter-accusation of lying and treason is made against a Point Adult and child. The Council—'

Hemminal had climbed up from the boat to whisper urgently in the King's ear. Not turning his head, Pyroonak interrupted, 'We must not act in haste. The Council will meet again at the next high tide.' He pointed to some Hunters. 'You four, guard them—'

'Four of Hemminal's own crew? Would the prisoners survive till the trial?' Prentastal interrupted. All round, breath hissed in disgust. 'And considering how hastily you decided to throw them out of Death Gate, King Pyroonak, I see no reason why we should delay now.' A mutter of agreement, a breeze of nodding heads rolled over the crowd.

Distom was whispering to his attendant, who straightened up and raised a hand. 'Point Father asks me to inform you that he has not, and will not try to link with his young sister to help her. I have attended him for the last two tides; I can vouch for this. He also suggests,' the Silver went on as the buzz of approval faded, 'that the meeting be held out here, now, where the whole City can watch, rather than in the Council Hall.'

The assembly muttered approval; this was how it should be, everything open, nothing hidden.

It didn't take long to get organized. Almost every soul in Atlantis was already out on the terraces and House roofs, squeezed into the harbour flat, climbing down into boats and up on to sheds to watch. White cushions were laid on the central stone bench in front of the Hunters' Halls for the King and Queen to sit side by side, pointedly ignoring each other, and rows of bone stools in a half-ring on each side and behind them for the Council. Point House gathered behind Distom and Point Mother, behind the youngsters on one side; Kelp House behind Hemminal opposite them.

Some Point women brought down fresh clothes for all three youngsters. Peter felt shy about changing in public, but his soaking ski-suit was cold and clinging. A rub with a rough towel warmed him, and the soft, baggy tunic and dry socks were wonderfully comfortable. 'Thankyoo,' he told the women. They nodded grimly. The tunic was two checked cavy-wool blankets hastily cobbled together, belted with a leather rope, but it would do for a Giant.

131

A Silver gave Mungith and Chooker a pain-stop pill each, and two for Peter, who took them gingerly, hiding his shock at the man's single eye. These small, glowing people seemed to be crazily different. He could see black and white, brown, red and yellow, plain and patchy skins and fur—fur? Yes. All over some of them. And tails, and pointed ears and teeth, and one with three arms. He shivered. But he mustn't offend them, especially the one who was trying to help. He made himself smile thanks.

'I'll see to your wounds after the hearing, if—eh, well, if—' The Silver stopped, flushing slightly. Chooker and Mungith exchanged glances. If it was worth while.

At last, the Priest of the Little Gods lifted the old horn and blew once more. It wasn't a good idea to disregard the Gods; sometimes they were watching closer than you expected—or hoped. The King rose, raising an arm towards the God Pillars in the centre of the Harbour. 'Beliyyak, God of men, hear us!'

'Beliyyak hear us!' the crowd repeated.

'I hear!' echoed towards them from the far wall of the cavern.

Prentastal turned to the right-hand pillar. 'Bastiyyal, Goddess of women, hear us!'

'Bastiyyal, hear us!'

'I hear!'

The Gods were listening. Even the birds fell silent.

15

Pyroonak stood up again, but Prentastal raised a hand. 'Let us save time. Chooker, Point First Daughter, Mungithak, Adult of Point House, tell us why you left the City, and what happened to you, and why you have brought this Giant back.'

Chooker peered muzzily up at Mungith. 'You tell them, Mungith. I . . . I can't.'

Mungith didn't feel any too wonderful himself, but he had to do his best. He blinked at her, and at Peter, and at his Family. What should he say?

Hemminal's freezing, burning eyes were fixed on him.

Was he afraid of her? Yes. Did he want her to run Atlantis? No.

Had he the courage to stop her?

This was no worse than diving among sharks. He pushed to his feet, took a deep breath and tore his eyes away from Hemminal's glare. 'Some days ago there was an accident in the boat—'

'Stop wasting time!' Hemminal interrupted quickly. 'You brought in the first Giant, that killed half the City. Now you're bringing more disease and death and destruction. Did the Council give you permission to go? No! Did you bring in another Giant? There it is! What more is there to say? All three must die! To save the City!'

Mungith expected uproar, but although Hemminal's crew, Kelp House, and the Wilders behind them all cheered, few others joined them. The Sensers had been using their skill to bring the crowd to reason. People had had time to calm down, consider that harpoon, remember what they knew of Hemminal.

'There is a great deal more to say!' Prentastal declared.

'What? That that Point brat accuses me of murder? What proof has she?'

Mungith didn't know what to say. He'd get no backing from the rest of the crew about Fixatchak's death. In the mine only Chooker had seen what happened, apart from the Wilders who couldn't testify even if they would. 'She saw you kill Giffaral—'

'Has she witnesses?' The Hunter sharpness of Hemminal's voice sliced at him like her own axe. 'No? Her word against mine, then. But without other witnesses or evidence, Custom says the Council must believe an Adult before a child!'

Mungith suddenly realized that he had really believed Chooker all along; he had just refused to accept it. Now, as it looked as if she was beaten, a fury of injustice roared in his chest till he could scarcely breathe, till he hardly noticed Chooker gripping his arm to pull herself to her feet beside him.

'Adult!' Chooker called into the resentful hush. 'I claim Adulthood!'

'Yes!' Behind her, Mother's jewellery jingled musically as she jumped up. 'Yes! She has that right!' she called dramatically. 'So she can accuse you, Hemminal! And we know whose word will be believed!' Beaming, she reseated herself with a toss of her flounces.

Hemminal sulked, head down, glowering out across the harbour, arms folded in obvious disgust, while Prentastal led Chooker through the short ceremony. 'Point House has lost a child,' she announced to the crowd. 'But it has gained an Adult; Chookeral!' She formally greeted the new Adult, palms up, palms down, and then hugged her, while Point House cheered defiantly. Many of the crowd took it up, stamping and clapping applause. Now justice could be done!

'Mungith . . . please—' Chooker murmured. She sank back on to her stool, jubilant. Hemminal couldn't stop her now! But Distom was frowning, uneasy. Something was wrong . . .

Hemminal straightened up, turned to face the crowd. Her eyes were slitted, her voice greasy with satisfaction. 'Chookeral, First Daughter of Point House, has insulted my honour. I challenge her to duel. To death. And by Custom, a challenge of honour must be dealt with before anything else.' She had trapped the little ratling very neatly!

A jeering, cheering shout rose from her friends. Everyone else stiffened in shock.

'Am I breaking Custom?' Hemminal sneered round the ring of appalled faces. Even Pyroonak looked stunned.

'Chooker is half your size!' Prentastal protested.

'Custom says nothing about that. She should have minded her Manners better.' Hemminal laughed. 'And I challenge Mungithak, Adult of Point House. And,' she gibed, 'I even challenge that freak of a Giant.' She drew her axe from its sling at her belt, and started to juggle with it, her teeth showing in a near-smile. 'To death.'

Mungith was stunned. A challenge from Hemminal? She'd kill him—kill them all . . .

'Duel? With Peter? But . . . but he hasn't been taught—he's only a boy! A child!' Chooker stuttered, ready to faint.

'He's big enough for two real people!' Hemminal sneered.

Hearing his name, Peter nudged Chooker. 'Wot shee want? Tawk too mee, Chooker!'

Chooker sighed. She hadn't the energy . . . Eh, somebody had to tell him. She concentrated fiercely on imaging Hemminal fighting her and Mungith and Peter, waving a knife in triumph over their bodies. 'Okay?' He blinked.

Prentastal pulled herself together. 'They are all exhausted and hurt. They may appoint a champion to fight on their behalf. Custom allows that.'

Hemminal laughed. 'Who'll fight for a Giant?'

'I will!' Mother shouted. 'I've won my fights!'

'Twenty years ago!' Hemminal sneered.

'I'll champion them!' Chooker's middle sister Motoral pushed furiously out from the crowd.

'You can't! Neither of you!' Pyroonak objected. 'Members of the Council may only duel each other. And people may only champion for their own House, and Motoral has been adopted into Cat House. They must find someone in Point House.'

No one in Point had ever fought a duel to more than first blood, not even the Weapons Teacher. Mungith stood up. His sight was blurred again, his hand was crippled and he was swaying, unsteady on his feet, but what else could he do? 'I'm not afraid!' He was, but . . . 'I'll fight!'

'You can't!' Mother was horrified. 'Not with half a hand!'

Peter was tugging at Chooker's arm. 'Shee want too fite? Fite yoo and Mungith and mee? Too deth? Too maik us ded?' Irritably, Chooker nodded. Why couldn't he be quiet?

To her astonishment, he grinned. Nervously, but definitely. 'Okay! I fite hur!'

'Yoo?' In astonishment Mungith swung round. 'Yoo can fite?'

'Yep. Ie can fite good,' Peter announced. Well, he'd had a fair chance of the Junior Championship. At last, here was something he could do well, something useful, instead of being herded along like a half-witted sheep.

Sceptical, Mungith gaped. Peter? Fight? Fight Hemminal?

Chooker blinked up at them both. Maybe . . . 'We've got to let him try,' she told Mungith. 'We don't know he can't— and Hemminal can beat anyone in Point. Even you.'

'Yes. Even me.' It hurt to admit it. 'While I'm hurt, anyway . . . '

In a glimpse of her normal snippiness, Chooker sniffed.

Gulping, Mungith declared the Giant's readiness to fight.

136

In any dispute between the King and Queen's own Houses, the Priest acted as judge. Now Shevirrak stated, 'As the one challenged, the Giant has choice of weapons.' Point House Hunters eagerly offered axes, a harpoon, an axe like Hemminal's, knives, but Peter waved them aside and held up his open hands. Wrestling? To death? Astonished and thrilled, the crowd started offering bets, the odds heavy against the Giant. Defiantly, on Distom's nod, the Points took them all.

Hemminal studied the young Giant carefully. He was a hand taller than she was, so he'd have a longer reach, but he was soft. She had never been beaten in wrestling, either formal matches or the vicious, deadly brawling of the Wilder Caves. He was a fool. Sneering, she tossed her axe to her cousin Wheerain, unpinned her blue glass soul-stone from her nose and handed it to the Priest, and gestured for the stools to be cleared away.

Peter gave Chooker his glasses and drew a deep breath. His teacher always said that tae kwon do could save your life. Now was the time to find out if it was true. This wasn't a grading, or even a tournament. This was really serious. He had to get it right. Don't fight unless you have to, his teacher said, but if you must fight, win. Yes, well. Don't quit.

He kicked off his socks to get good footing on the rock, and began some warm-up exercises. A pulled muscle from starting cold wouldn't help. The pills had cured all the pain in his toes and legs. He had had almost three hours' rest in the boat, and a refreshing swim. He didn't feel bad at all. Concentrate on bringing balance to the centre. It wasn't usual before a match, but he did a few practice patterns of moves to still his nerves, help centre himself. His opponent was staring—ignore her. What techniques would she have? Calm. He'd find out. He'd see her off! No, not that way. Calm. Balance at the centre. Do the t'oi gye pattern again, in agitation he'd made a mess of it. He must guard his right

137

hand, the bones were almost mended but it still hurt, she'd see the bandage and go for it—leave that for now. Concentrate. Calm. Balance. Strong spirit. Calm.

The whole of Atlantis watched as he bent and stretched, punched and kicked the air. 'Courting dodo-cock!' Hemminal jeered.

Chooker gripped Mungith's hand. 'This isn't just prancing about,' she whispered.

'Uhuh,' Mungith grunted. 'He knows what he's doing. Maybe he can really fight?'

At last Peter stopped, relaxed and still-faced. He breathed deeply five times, bowed to the King and Queen, bowed to Hemminal, walked into the middle of the open area and stood ready.

Experienced in duels, Hemminal stalked round him to throw him off stance, snarling, stamping, jeering, making him shift round to keep facing her, and suddenly screamed in his face. When he jumped back, she barked a laugh, set her feet firm and held out her splayed right hand for the normal starting grip. Nobody had ever beaten her. Nobody would.

Peter knew he was expected to take the hand, but that was her style, not his. He mustn't let her grip him. She must be as strong as the people in the mine; even if she was six inches shorter than him, she'd tear him apart—stop that! Calm. Balance. Strong spirit. He poised, bouncing on the balls of his feet, knees bent, ready to move in any direction. Tempt her to attack. He reached forward . . .

He didn't know how to fight properly! Snorting contempt, Hemminal grabbed for the hand waving unsteadily in front of her face. Her own hand was knocked aside; fingers stabbed towards her eyes. As she recoiled her front knee was kicked out from under her and she fell. She rolled up fast away from a kicking, but the Giant had danced back. How did he do that?

Chooker yelled in delight at the sudden upset. She had scarcely seen the flicker of Peter's hands, he was so fast! 'Peter! Okay, Peter!' Mungith joined her. 'Okay, Peter, okay, Peter!' Mother waved to the Points to join in, clapping and stamping rhythmically. 'Okay, Peter, okay, Peter!' Whatever it meant, it encouraged their champion.

On the other side of the fighting ground Wilders were clustering behind the Kelps and Hemminal's crew, pressing forward. 'Hem-min-al! Hem-min-al!'

While the two fighters circled each other, all round them feet and hands began to beat out one or other rhythm. Most were the triple beat for Hemminal, but not a few joined the steady one-two-three-four of the Points. No one else was chanting yet; they hadn't decided who to shout for.

Easing her knee, Hemminal moved in again, more wary. He had one foot well forward; she snatched at the tempting knee. It wasn't there; somehow the foot kicked the side of her head, an elbow jabbed the side of her neck—but she was already leaping back. To her amazement the Giant followed her, kicking as much as hitting, never letting her get a hold, driving her back and back with flying hands and feet. She ducked and dodged wildly, just twisting aside from the edge of the quay, blocking or fending off blows more by chance than judgement, dazzled by the speed of the attack.

Peter was getting annoyed with himself. Yes, it was hard to judge distance in the dim, shadowless light, and it was disconcerting to fight someone who didn't react to his moves as his usual opponents did, but he should still do better than this! He was just sparring, pulling his punches as he'd have done in practice. This was for real! Come on, dozy, wake up, punch through, not to! But it felt wrong to try to damage a smaller, older woman, even though he knew she'd hurt him if she could. Especially when she hadn't landed a blow yet, and he knew he could beat her—

She caught his right hand and wrenched it. The half-mended bones stabbed and cracked. Yelling, at first in pain and then to keep his mind off it, Peter drove an elbow into Hemminal's ribs, managed to twist out of her fist and backed off, nursing his hand. Jeez, it hurt! That would teach him to get cocky! He couldn't use it, he'd lost that hand— stop that. Calm. Balance.

Hemminal was rubbing her side, grinning. It was worth it; she was sure the monster's right hand was out of action now. If she could corner him, she'd get him!

Peter's best move was still to attack, kicking to stay at a distance, keeping out of Hemminal's grasp. She was forced back, dodging, ducking, snatching, falling twice, once unexpectedly throwing herself towards him so that he just managed to skip out of reach of her clutching hands. He was winning; one solid kick would do it. If he could keep it up.

They both paused for breath for a moment. Hemminal felt angrily frustrated—not afraid, but . . . The Giant wasn't fighting properly, jiggling about like an eel, making her look a fool! She couldn't catch a hold anywhere, never mind on the bad hand. But she was learning how he fought. At his next front kick, she slapped up his foot, throwing him backwards. Peter tried for a rolling break-fall, but the rock was harder and less even than a mat; he landed awkwardly, the breath knocked from his lungs, and took a fraction of a second longer than he should to get up. Hemminal hurled herself after him, grabbed his ankle and heaved him scrabbling towards her. Got him!

As he had feared, she was enormously powerful. He kicked and writhed, but couldn't break free. Her boots kicked him, stamped mercilessly on his right hand. She dropped on him, her knees nearly breaking his spine. Somehow he squirmed on to his back, just foiling a neck-breaker grip. She laughed and sat across his stomach.

Callused and wiry, her hands settled round his throat like the jaws of a Moray eel.

Peter could barely move for the pain of his back and his broken hand. He couldn't breathe. He couldn't wriggle free. His heartbeat pounded, drummed in his head. His lungs were on fire. He was weakening, dying . . .

Losers don't try, winners don't quit.

His left hand clawed feebly up her arm.

Hemminal ignored it; it couldn't hurt her.

He tickled her armpit.

She jumped. For a fraction of a second her weight moved, her hands slackened.

Desperately Peter heaved, shoved, and kicked her off him. Breath whooping into his chest, he staggered to his feet, coughing, more than half crippled, his head spinning.

Surprised, Hemminal sat and laughed out loud. 'Clever boy!'

Peter knew he couldn't go on. He had to finish it soon . . . or she would.

Hemminal was enjoying herself now. She was tougher, stronger than he was. She'd have him . . . She took her time rising to her feet, like a cat playing with a rat.

Suddenly she realized the crowd were shouting, not just stamping. And not for her. The Points, the Coals, all who knew Hemminal or were impressed by the young Giant's skill and courage, more and more of the City were cheering for Peter, mentally sending him encouragement and strength. 'Okay Peter okay Peter!' She paused to snarl defiance at them.

Only vaguely aware of the words, Peter found that the stamping and clapping, the steady booming crash and thud somehow blanked out fear, blanked out pain, urged him on. Never give in. Balance. Strong spirit. Calm. Think. What hadn't he tried?

He turned his back.

He was trying to run! Hemminal leapt forward to grab his bad hand and tug him back. The monster wouldn't get away like that—she'd break his neck—

Peter had her in the corner of his eye, judging distance . . . Now! Back kick to the stomach—good—roundhouse kick to the head—a hit, but not solid—one-knuckle strike with his good left hand between the eyes—misjudged it, she was doubled over, stumbling backwards, and he almost broke his fingers on her skull.

Snarling, she hurtled back to attack.

Don't quit.

Yelling in pain and defiance, he launched himself in a flying side kick to the head—

He was too tired, too slow. She jerked aside. He missed her completely.

As he landed Hemminal caught and wrenched his left arm. Even before the pain, he heard the pop of his shoulder dislocating. She twisted it, forced him to his knees before her.

Both hands gone.

Hissing in triumph, relishing the moment, Hemminal leisurely reached for his neck again.

She wasn't going to hurt him; she was going to kill him.

With his last strength, Peter forced his broken right hand into the spear shape and struck blindly upwards. The pain shattered him. He didn't know where the blow landed.

16

Eventually the agony faded enough for Peter to open his eyes.

Hemminal was lying still in front of him, crumpled, snoring as she breathed. Her throat was already one huge crimson swelling where his hand had smashed into her Adam's apple. Faces gaped at him all round, intent and silent.

'Kill her!' Point Mother screamed at him. 'You must kill her! Kill her!' The crowd joined in, with stabbing, kicking, wringing gestures.

Peter peered round. What did they want?

Mungith ran forward. You mustn't touch a duellist until the fight was declared over, but he knelt facing Peter, shouting urgently. 'Peter! Peter, Hemminal say fite too ded. Noh stop now! You get hur ded. Gowon! Now!'

Kill her? While she was out cold? 'Noh! Noh way! Noh!' Unsteady and weak, Peter shook his head so hard he almost fell.

Leave her alive, to recover and kill him? 'Giants are crazy!' Mungith yelled. He looked round for help. The shouting died away in confusion and uncertainty.

'One must kill the other,' Priest Shevirrak declared. 'It is Custom.'

'He won't do it!' Chooker called. 'He thinks killing is wrong!'

In the awkward pause, Distom's soft voice could just be heard. 'If you stop the duel, we can hear the accusations against Hemminal. There would be no point if she is dead.'

The Priest nodded in relief. 'Yes, eh, yes! Thank you, Point Father, a good thought. If the Giant can rise to his feet unaided, we will accept that he is the victor. H'm? Yes.'

'Getup, Peter!' Mungith urged. 'Getup!' Other voices joined in. 'Getup Peter, getup Peter!' More and more, louder and louder, stamping and clapping, cheering.

What? Why? He couldn't . . . but winners don't quit. A last effort—

Trembling, groaning with the strain, Peter forced himself up. What now?

At last the Priest nodded. A rush of people, Mungith, Chooker, Silvers, half of Point House surrounded Peter, supporting him, holding him as his wavery legs melted and he fell and fell and fell into a whirling black hole.

Half an hour later the open space had shrunk to only a couple of paces wide as the crowd pressed forward, flowing round the benches where the Giant and Hemminal had been laid. All eyes were on King Pyroonak, facing the Priest and Prentastal and the Council, his face patchy red and white with shame and anger. 'I didn't know Giffaral was murdered,' he claimed. 'Hemminal said she had been killed in the flood. I believed her!'

Silver Mother, the strongest Senser in the City, was touching his shoulder to check his mind. She nodded confirmation. 'Yes . . . er . . . yes. That's true. It was Hemminal who did the . . . er . . . the killing. Her mind was full of triumph about it. And . . . er . . . pleasure.' She made a face of disgust. Prying into Hemminal's semi-concious mind for the truth had been like diving in a sewer full of rats. Pyroonak's face showed his relief—and his chagrin as she went on, 'But . . . er . . . the King did not ask too much. He was afraid he would hear what he didn't want to know.'

Shevirrak, seated on the Royal bench beside Prentastal, frowned severely. Priests seldom did more than keep the stock of soul-stones, sound the high-tide horn, and check on earthquake pressures; very, very few had the thrill of judging a King. Secretly he was rather enjoying himself. He couldn't let it show, of course. 'But you did plan to break the mine. And you lied to the Council, and persuaded Granite Father to lie also, to make us think the flood was far worse than it was. You said that it threatened all the Coalmines and to keep it clear the Queen must go to the Gods at once.'

Granite Father, defensive on his bench, protested bitterly. 'I didn't lie, Priest Shevirrak! I—well, I exaggerated a little, and made the most of what my Miners told me—but I didn't lie!'

'You didn't tell the truth, either!' Point Mother called, to a general mutter of disgust.

'The Queen was planning to ruin Atlantis!' Pyroonak protested. He looked round for support. 'Point House killed half the City, bringing in the first Giant—and think, what will happen now they've done it again? I only wanted the good of the City!'

'Was it good for the City to insult the Gods by using them in your schemes?' Under the tall peak of her copper and jet head-dress, Point Mother's face was flushed with anger. 'What decent Gods would want people to lie and cheat and kill in their names? You wanted no one to argue with you, that's what you wanted! Power for yourself, your ideas! You rotten kelp-stem, you always—'

'Point Mother, please!' With some difficulty the Priest silenced her. 'King Pyroonak, good intentions are no excuse for evil actions. A reason, maybe, but not an excuse.'

He paused; a Silver was leading the young Giant forward through the crowd, guiding him to a stool beside the two Point youngsters.

'Hi, Peter. Okay?' Mungith whispered.

'Okay!' Peter confirmed. Oddly enough, it was true. When he woke, he found his shoulder joint was back in place and working. The one-eyed medicine man had been gently massaging his broken right hand, and he found he could actually move his fingers. To his amazement he didn't hurt, not anywhere. He even felt quite alert. These people were good doctors! 'Yoo okay?'

Mungith nodded. He and Chooker were tired, of course, after telling their story, but the pain-stops, and the excitement of the fight, hadn't worn off yet.

'Is the Giant fit to speak to us?' the Priest asked. 'Can you think to him?'

The Silver grimaced. 'I could, eh, yes, I have tried, but I feel . . . Giants' minds are . . . Remember Bil.' The other Sensers nodded agreement. 'I . . . er . . . believe Point First Daughter Chookeral would do it better. Yes indeed.' He nodded, fussy as Silvers tended to be. 'If she feels well enough.'

'Can we accept that?' the Priest asked, glancing round the rows of Mothers and Fathers. There was a clear, if grudging, majority for trusting the Point girl. 'Point First Daughter, will you make contact with the Giant for us?'

Reluctantly, Chooker bowed. As she straightened, her head spun; pain-stops didn't cure dizziness. Seeing her waver, Mungith whispered, 'Go on, Chook! You can do it!' Encouragement wafted from Distom, sitting behind her. Yes, she could manage.

She took Peter's hand and calmed her mind to link with him. He smiled, and his mind slid into tune with hers as if they were in the same Family. Either he was getting better at it or she was. Or both, of course.

'Why did he come here?' the Priest asked. 'No, don't just tell us—ask him, now.'

Peter grinned, his face as cheeky as his schoolteachers had ever seen it. 'For fun!' he said, and Chooker grinned faintly back as she caught the meaning and translated it.

'He is only a child,' Distom commented quietly. 'Our First Daughter felt something the same. It was an adventure. Giant children seem to act very like normal ones.' Shark

146

Father snorted scornfully, but there were a few answering smiles.

'If your people and ours meet, can we trust you large people not to try to hurt us, kill us with your terrible weapons?'

Peter's serious face and the pause before he answered made it clear that he was thinking about it hard. 'Most of them,' Chooker reported. 'But there will be some bad ones, he says. But even they'll try to cheat us more than kill us, he thinks. We'd just have to be careful. Bil said the same.'

'We remember, thank you,' Pearl Mother commented, her tone freezing. 'How many bad ones does he himself know?'

That took some time to express. 'Not many really bad ones,' Chooker said. 'Doctormurry, at the Giant's House that I—we—were in, he's nasty. He tried to take credit for what Bil had done. Quite a lot of them exaggerate or cheat like that, or worse, especially the . . . the Kings and Queens who run their Cities and Caves. I don't understand how that can be allowed, but . . . but apart from some of his friends at Lessons, and I think that was just a joke, Peter doesn't know any personally.'

'He is just a boy. He might not know them well,' Shark Father suggested.

'They are clearly not all like that, though. And bullies and liars are not unknown here.' Point Mother's eye was sharp on Pyroonak and Father Granite. 'We have no choice, anyway. We must meet with the Giants now. We must send the boy back, at least.' There was a heavy, reluctant silence.

The Priest whispered with the Council, in a shimmer of waving hands and nodding head-dresses. At last he stood up. 'I am ready to give judgement. May the Little Gods watch over us, to see that it is fair.' The usual addition, 'But not too closely', was not fitting here.

Shevirrak pointed first to Peter. 'The boy Giant is brave, and has helped, not harmed us. He will be returned to his

Family, with gifts from Point House to thank him for fighting for the Points who were also challenged. Is it fair?'

Point Mother and Distom bowed approval. 'It is fair.'

'Only the best. Samples,' Mother breathed, aside.

'Teach your toes to twiddle,' Distom murmured, already planning.

Her lips twitched. 'Sorry.'

Mungith smiled to Peter. 'Yoo goh bak too scotbais, too Annabel,' he whispered.

Peter sighed in relief, though he hadn't been afraid he'd have to stay. Not really . . .

'Granite Father, you used half-truths and exaggeration to harm Queen Prentastal. At the next Council meeting you will apologize in person and in public to her, and beg her pardon. You will pay half your teeth in atonement, half to her personally, half to the Royal House to be used to help those in need. Granite House will also pay a third of its store of teeth to the Royal House.' The Priest looked him full in the face. 'Is it fair?'

Granite Father's pale skin was scarlet with fury and embarrassment under the high green box of his head-dress. His actions had lost Granite House an enormous amount of respect. With that, and the large fine on his House, he would be very unpopular, and might well be deposed. But no one from Granite had argued about the exaggeration he had given to their reports. They were due to pay something, too. Grudging, he nodded. 'It is fair.' The crowd echoed him, clapping approval.

'Now, King Pyroonak!' As the Priest called him, the tall man in white stood forward, defensively stiff under the accusing eyes. 'You, our King, the leader of the City, you have betrayed the Little Gods and us all. The King must be a man of honour. You are not.'

Pyroonak flushed deep red, but old Shevirrak's thin voice was clear and cold as he went on relentlessly. 'Pyroonak,

King of Atlantis, for dishonouring the Gods and deceiving the City you are cast down from your place. Pyroonak, Adult of Kelp House, for scheming to cause the Queen's death you will give all of your teeth, half for Queen Prentastal herself, half to the Royal House. For plotting with your sister to break the mine, and for hiding the truth about the death of Giffaral, Adult of Coal House, you are declared Wilder.' He glanced round the crowd. 'Is it fair?' The Council nodded agreement; the crowd murmured in satisfaction. Who could ever trust him again? It was fair.

Pyroonak—now Pyroon—glared at the children, and the Giant. If it hadn't been for them . . .

Silver Mother touched his wrist. *Don't blame them, nor Hemminal. No one forced you. You chose. An Adult is responsible for his own actions. Is it not fair?*

He glared at her, too, but after a moment his eyes fell. He drew a deep breath, and bowed assent. 'It is fair. I was wrong to act as I did.' He had to force out the words, but the Silver's nod showed that they were sincere. Slowly, reluctantly, he took off his ivory coronet and handed it to the Priest. He raised a hand to remove his soul-stone, for Wilders did not keep them—and then his head rose and his jaw firmed. 'But I will not become a Wilder. I will go down into the Whirlies, to Beliyyak, and try to do better in my next life.'

An indrawn breath and murmur of surprise ran round the Harbour. He refused the disgrace and violence of life as a Wilder. Some people clapped gently in respect.

Shevirrak interrupted the buzz. 'No!' he declared. 'Only men of honour go to the Whirlies. He has been declared Wilder. He is not worthy to return to Beliyyak!'

To Mungith's surprise Prentastal looked vexed and sad, rather than pleased by the verdict. 'I hope, Pyroonak—Pyroon—that you will find a way to return to us in restored honour and trust.'

149

Pyroon could not meet her eyes. He was no longer flushed, but as white as his tunic. Slowly he removed his crystal soul-stone, placed it in Shevirrak's firmly outstretched hand, and dragged himself over to join the group of Wilders clustered behind Hemminal's bench.

The Priest beckoned Mungith and Chooker to step forward together. 'Mungithak, Point Adult, you went Outside not of your own will, but to save your cousin. You did not deliberately bring this Giant into the City. You have acted responsibly, with honour and courage, as is expected of an Adult.' The Council, even Shark Father, were nodding gravely. Mungith felt an odd mixture of pleasure at the mild praise, and deflation that he wasn't commended more strongly.

The Priest was not finished. 'However, you also deliberately used double words, allowing an untruth to spread to cover the killing of Fixatchak, Adult of Granite House. Out of loyalty to your leader, we know, but a reason is not always an excuse. But you have lost two fingers through the action of a Granite, so you have already paid something. Mungithak, Adult of Point House, you will give the Royal House one-third of all the teeth you won while hunting with Hemminal. You may keep the rest, and any profit that Point Father has made in trading for you. Each member of Hemminal's crew will give two-thirds, in the same way. Is it fair?'

From Hemminal's crew, packed round the bench where she lay, there was a snarl of annoyance and some muffled cursing, but Mungith bowed acceptance. 'It is fair.' Not as good as he had hoped, not as bad as he had feared. He had lost much of his year's work and wealth, but he'd recover. Chooker touched his good hand to pass him a little comfort, and the tiny warmth cheered him. He turned his hand to catch her fingers. Her turn next . . .

'Chookeral, Point First Daughter. Your case is more

serious. In childish conceit you acted against what you knew were the wishes of the Council. We have yet to see whether your action will bring benefits to Atlantis, as you and some others believe, or disaster; but the risk was not yours to take. Your witnessing a murder was chance. True, your action in returning promptly at some risk to yourself has saved a monstrous injustice. However, it was no more than your duty to your House. On the whole, you have not acted as an Adult should.'

He paused. Chooker realized what he was going to say. Mungith, who didn't, started to splutter, 'You're not going to declare her a Wilder! You can't!'

'Quiet!' The Priest was normally a meek little man, but this one time, imperious with command, his voice snapped Mungith's mouth shut. 'Point First Daughter, your recognition as an Adult is cancelled. You are still a child, and will have to take a full Adult Trial in due time, after at least a year. It should be one of work and judgement, not of daring or endurance.'

Prentastal considered. 'I might set her to teach a class of Kelp children Manners for a couple of sixty-tides.'

Chooker's jaw dropped in horror. Teach Kelps, after ruining their heroes Hemminal and Pyroon?

Kelp Mother nodded. 'I'd be glad to see her, Queen Prentastal.' Just how she meant it, no one could say.

'Now, we must deal with the last, and worst. Hemminal.' The Priest waved the crowd back, to clear a space between him and Hemminal's bench. Obediently, the people who had inched forward pressed back.

The bench was empty. Hemminal was gone. The other members of her crew had vanished with her, and Pyroon, and the Wilders who had squeezed forward behind them.

Beyond the bulk of the Royal House several people were hurrying into the entrance of the Wilders' Caves, right at the end of the cavern, a white tunic among the huddle, carrying something long and heavy. Hemminal had returned to her old friends.

'I give judgement.' The Priest's voice was clear in the silence. 'For striking Fixatchak, Adult of Granite House, to cause his death, for lying, and for causing others to lie to protect her, Hemminal, Adult of Kelp House, is declared Wilder, and all her teeth are forfeit. Kelp House, which raised Pyroon and Hemmin so badly, will also give half its teeth to the Royal House.'

Young Kelp Mother sighed; she had more troubles than enough already. Kelp Father looked furious. The fine was not unexpected, and would not be much. Kelp was not a rich House, and Hemmin had brought in most of their teeth anyway.

Shevirrak was not finished. 'For the deliberate murder of Giffaral, Adult of Coal House, Hemmin, Wilder, is declared Outcast. She will be seized on sight, and thrust out from Death Gate. Her soul-stone is disgraced. Her name will never be spoken in friendship again.' He stared round challengingly. 'Is it fair?'

A low mutter of agreement rose from the crowd, even the sullen Kelps. 'It is fair.'

The Priest turned out towards the God Pillars, and called, 'Is it fair?'

Everyone shouted the question after him. 'Is it fair?'

The booming echo reassured them. 'Fair.'

The Priest held out the blue glass soul-stone Hemmin had given him so that everyone could see it. He dropped it, and amid a growl of approval disdainfully ground it under his sandal till it cracked and powdered. If Pyroon ever did redeem himself, he could reclaim his soul-stone. In any case it would be used again, when he had been dead long enough to be forgotten, but not this one; Hemmin would never be reborn.

Suddenly losing the righteousness that had vitalized him,

152

the Priest shrank to his normal insignificant self, his skinny neck bobbing inside his heavy embroidered collar. 'Er . . . isn't that all?'

'Thank you, Priest Shevirrak.' Prentastal raised her voice slightly. 'Tomorrow the Council will meet to choose a new King. May the Little Gods watch over us all—but not too closely.'

Mother leaned forward to give Chooker and Mungith a huge hug, tears in her eyes, before hurrying over to speak to Prentastal. The Mothers and Fathers rose, nodded to Prentastal, and gathered up their cushions. People began to drift gradually homewards, excitedly discussing and acting out the fight, staring at the Giant, arguing, paying off bets. Point House had done well.

Chooker sagged. It was over—well, more or less. She tried to smile to Peter. 'Wee okay now. Wee goh too—' she gestured up to the triangular golden windows of Point House, above them.

'Home?' Peter said. 'Yoor home up thair?'

Touching his wrist, she felt the comfortable, loving meaning of the word. 'Home,' she confirmed. 'Wee goh home.'

'Wot abowt mee?' Peter asked.

'Timorra. I goh with yoo home too scotbais timorra.' Mungith sighed, but it had to be done, and he was the only one who knew the way and was fit enough to go. He glanced at Mother, talking eagerly with Prentastal and Distom further up the quay, and raised his eyebrows to Chooker. 'I wonder what's so important.'

Chooker was so tired that she could hardly stay upright. She knew, intimately, all in the tight little group. Effortlessly, their words slid into her mind. 'Prentast's saying we'll need to watch out, Hemmin will cause trouble again. Distom says he'd rather like to go Outside and try trading with the Giants. Mother's nearly having a fit.

Prentast suggests Giant Doctors may know a cure for Distom's weakness. Mother's calming down. Distom asks who'd run Point House trade while he's gone. Mother says you can try your hand at it while she can keep an eye on you, it'll be good practice for when you're—oh.' She suddenly jumped awake and blushed. 'I shouldn't be listening like this.'

Mungith regarded her with awe. 'I didn't know you were that good! Nobody's that good!' He felt breathless. Had she really been going to say, 'When you're Point Father'? Was she really planning to marry him? Still? After all he had said to her? With all the others she could choose from? He mustn't push it, though. Better pretend he hadn't noticed.

'It just came to me. Don't tell anybody, Mung,' Chooker begged him. Thank Bastiyyal he hadn't noticed that she was planning to marry him—his hair would puff to triple size. Well, when it grew again it would. She made herself smile. 'K'mawn, Peter! Wee goh home!'

'Okay!' Peter grinned. He was just starting to realize that he'd done something rather more important even than winning a Championship. He reached to help her to her feet, and to his surprise found Mungith's hand there first. Their three hands linked, and they found themselves laughing, in relief and release from fear. Their three voices chorused the same words.

'Wee all okay now!'